"Behind me."

Nicole startled, tightening her grip on the thick leash hooked to the dog's harness.

Waffles's growl deepened.

Troy didn't wait for her to move. Fear claimed Nicole, so he shuffled in front instead. He wasn't much of a shield but he was better than nothing.

"What is it?" Nicole whispered, bunching the back of his shirt.

"I don't know." Troy kept his gun pointed at the ground, ready to pull the trigger. "It's too quiet. Something's off."

Adrenaline coursed through his veins, sharpening Troy's sight, sound and smell. Instincts screamed he needed to hide Nicole, but where? What was the threat?

A muted crack echoed just as his right front tire rocked.

Troy whirled, grabbing Nicole, dragging her to the other side of the truck. A bullet couldn't penetrate the engine block. Waffles growled and barked, fighting against the sudden new direction.

The truck rocked again, just as another muted shot echoed in the breeze.

"Sniper rifle with a suppressor," Troy announced. "He's shooting out my tires."

P.A. DePaul resides outside Philadelphia in the US. In her free time, you can find her reading, working on a puzzle, playing with her dog, winning game nights against her husband (sometimes) or whipping up something in the kitchen. You can learn more about her at padepaul.com, Facebook.com/padepaul and Instagram.com/padepaul.

Deadly Mountain Treasure

P.A. DePAUL

LOVE INSPIRED
INSPIRATIONAL ROMANCE

LOVE INSPIRED®
INSPIRATIONAL ROMANCE

ISBN-13: 978-1-335-42619-2

Deadly Mountain Treasure

Copyright © 2022 by Penni DePaul

Recycling programs
for this product may
not exist in your area.

For questions and comments about the quality of this book, please contact us
at CustomerService@Harlequin.com.

Love Inspired
22 Adelaide St. West, 41st Floor
Toronto, Ontario M5H 4E3, Canada
www.LoveInspired.com

Printed in U.S.A.

And he said unto them, Take heed, and beware of covetousness: for a man's life consisteth not in the abundance of the things which he possesseth.
—*Luke* 12:15

This book is dedicated to Johanna Raisanen.
You are amazing.

Acknowledgments

A huge thank-you goes to my husband. He's a sounding board, brainstormer and rock star at keeping the household running while I'm writing.

Massive squishy hugs go to my agent, Michelle Grajkowski. Her support and dedication keep this author on the sane side of life. (Sort of. She tries her best.)

Colossal thank-yous belong to my editor, Johanna Raisanen. She's the reason this book turned out amazing IMHO.

I don't even know where to begin on the thank-you scale for Rich Worthington and the Lower Moreland Police Department. Rich, your willingness to answer my barrage of emails, calls, texts and popping in the station is beyond appreciated. Thank you. Thank you. Thank you.

Thank you to Lauri Bowen-Vaccare for answering my questions about dogs and training. Mwah!

Pat McGee and Tom Moore, I thank you for helping me with the technical aspects of the construction equipment. I took liberties with the cab dimensions. That's totally on me!

My final thank-you belongs to you, the reader. I appreciate the support and your time in reading this labor of love. It means the world to me.

Chapter One

Tears dropped into the hole at the same time Nicole Witten's shovel bit into the dirt. A sob wrenched from her soul as she stomped on the top of the metal scoop to dig deeper into the ground.

Why? she railed, muscling the wooden handle to leverage the fresh soil onto the nearby growing pile. White and pink flower petals littered the area from the tangle of six-foot, overgrown mountain laurel bushes. A wooden bench had once rested peacefully beside them, but not anymore. The shrubs had long ago warped and claimed it.

Stabbing the shovel back into the cavity, she gripped the worn wood and rested her forehead on her uncle's work gloves.

Gone. How could Uncle Ross be gone? The fifty-six-year-old boisterous man had so much life raging inside him, he should've lived forever.

Memories assaulted her, dragging her deeper into despair. A collage of the summers blended, offering her glimpses of laughter, tears, daredevil stunts, and fascinating lessons. From the time she was six, Uncle Ross and Aunt Suzanne had taken her in from the last day of school to the end of August. At thirty-one now, she had a lifetime of experiences wrapped in the two-story house and vast tract of forested land in the Pocono Mountains.

"It's not real," she whispered. "It *can't* be real." Tears clogged her throat, causing a lump to stick in its base. She had no warning. No indication he'd die of a heart attack. Three weeks ago he'd collapsed on this spot, digging near the roots she now attacked.

"God." She raised her face to the blue, sunny sky. "Why did You have to take both Witten men?" First her father when she was two years old, now her uncle. "I needed them."

Aunt Suzanne had passed away six years ago, and now with Uncle Ross gone, Nicole had only her mother left. Technically, she wasn't completely alone, but she and her mother had never gotten along. Her loud and energetic uncle took her fishing, cleaned her skinned knees, and taught her how to climb rocks. He told outrageous stories and kept her company when she had a nightmare. He invented riddles for her to solve that led to prizes and treasures. He encouraged her to become a dental hygienist when her mother kept pushing Nicole to follow in her footsteps and choose real estate as a career. Uncle Ross had been her rock, her surrogate parent, her everything…and now he was gone.

Tears flowed, mingling with the sweat. The unusually warm, mid-June day should've had the two of them hiking through the forest to his favorite fishing spot. Not her alone, attacking overgrown bushes in the hope it quieted the grief swallowing her whole.

The house stifled her. Ross permeated every surface, stealing her ability to breathe. The man wasn't the best housekeeper, he put off—ignored—a lot of maintenance, and the decor hadn't been updated for as long as Nicole could remember. But none of that dampened the love and warmth etched into the walls.

Jamming her cross-trainer on the back of the metal scoop, she strangled the wooden handle. "Why?" she growled, throwing the dirt onto the pile. "Why him?" she snapped at God. "Why now?"

Another load hit the heap.

"I loved—" She choked. Past tense. *It's not right.*

Dirt flew to the growing mound. "I should've had more time." She *needed* more time. Didn't God understand that?

Didn't He care? Pain gripped her heart, and she sobbed at the loss. Tears blurred the widening trench.

"We should be tackling this together." She jabbed the shovel downward, unable to see anything. He had already started. She just continued where he left off. If he stood across from her now, he'd ask about her job and chide her on her lack of dating. His favorite new subject.

Another pang squeezed her heart, and she cried out, bending over.

He'd never give her advice again. Never tease her about finding the right man to marry so he'd stop worrying. Never present her with riddles to solve—not true. He'd left one last one with his will, but she hadn't had the heart to do more than skim the single sheet of paper.

And he'd never have the opportunity to tell her she'd inherit everything.

"I need *you*, not the house," she wheezed.

Uncle Ross had left her his entire estate. Debt free. No mortgage. No outstanding liens. No overdue property taxes. In fact, he'd established an account with a local attorney to pay for everything pertaining to the estate for the next ten years in the event of his death. Her jaw had hit the floor. Uncle Ross never seemed like a rich man. Sure, he was once a successful attorney in Chicago, but he'd retired and moved to Bell Edge twenty-four years ago. He'd never taken the Pennsylvania bar exam to reestablish his practice. He'd been happy with the occasional part-time job throughout the years.

After that fateful day in the attorney's office, she severed her apartment lease in Maryland, packed her entire life into cardboard boxes, and moved to Bell Edge. Her lucrative career had her living comfortably, but she left it anyway. She needed to be as close to her uncle as possible. With the man gone, she only had memories, and this place held many of the best.

Grinding the shovel into the hole, she resumed digging. She always thought she'd be married before she'd own a home and property this large, but her uncle had other ideas. Luckily, her savings account allowed her to take time off, and she needed it. Settling the estate, taking on the neglect, and clearing out the house was a full-time job. Add in tackling the unruly vegetation from the surrounding forest supplanting the designated yard, and she had her hands full.

The metal tip *thunked* into something, forcing her to stop. Letting go of the handle, it fell to the side as she dropped to her knees. Rich, moist soil coated her bare legs as she peered into the deep hole.

Blurry nothingness. Sniffling hard, she snatched both gloves off and wiped her wet face with sweaty hands. Rubbing her palms against the back of her athletic shorts, she blinked into the hole.

Chunks of rotting wood littered the space along with thick stalks of bush roots. Slapping her left hand on the ground, she bent, having to submerse almost her entire upper half. Studying the fragments closer, the wood didn't come from the vegetation. Scraping a piece with her fingernail, she found it hard like the lumber sold in home improvement stores or used in shipping crates.

That didn't make sense. Frowning, she hoisted herself up and marched to the shed. The hand-built structure held a hodgepodge of new and old stuff. Sometime in the last year, Ross had purchased a metal detector like the ones she'd seen on the beach. Maybe he'd developed a passion for uncovering arrowheads or Civil War artifacts. He also had an array of vintage gardening equipment in every shape and size. Snatching a few items off the cobwebbed pegboard wall, she crossed the distance to the tangle of bushes she had yet to tame. Along the way her gaze strayed to four other large disturbed patches strewn throughout the backyard. Her uncle hated the manual labor of landscaping, hence the overgrown vegetation everywhere, but he had made an effort lately.

Her grip tightened on a hand shovel. If he'd stuck to his aversion, he wouldn't have had a heart attack.

Late-afternoon sunlight caressed her exposed skin as she painstakingly cleared the dirt away. An hour later, her muscles begged her to stop, and her neck might never recover from the awkward position.

Her efforts were rewarded with a grimy white cloth amid the wood and dirt.

Tossing the small shovel aside, she grasped the sheet and lifted. Something metallic clanged within, and she slowed her ascent. Adjusting her grip to balance the weight, she lifted the item the rest of the way out.

Setting the bundle on the ground beside her, she stared at it. What could possibly be buried in her uncle's backyard? Had he known about it? Was that why he started digging in this spot?

Her hands trembled for some unknown reason as she gently unwound the sheet.

Chapter Two

Bell Edge, Pennsylvania, presented itself like a warm and fuzzy painting attracting tourists from all over. Nestled within Pocono Mountain peaks, it boasted an active downtown filled with quaint shops, eateries, art galleries, and small parks. A dedicated scenic railroad complete with a beautiful station carted passengers on a journey to show off the forest, rivers, caves, wild animals, and natural wonders.

The Witten property rested higher in the mountain, to the right of the bustling epicenter. From the front, glimpses of downtown buildings blended among the tree canopy. The back had vistas of majestic stone, flourishing trees, and lush vegetation. Prime real estate for a nature lover.

The whole area was a balm Bell Edge Police Detective Troy Hollenbeck desperately needed.

The first ten years of his law enforcement career, he spent in Philadelphia working his way up to homicide detective, but his last case had gone terribly wrong. Unable to stay another minute, he'd transferred two months ago. This Mayberry-like world shouldn't have executions and senseless violence. With a population around thirty-eight hundred, his days were now filled with civil complaints, the occasional disturbing the peace, low-level drug usage, and thefts thrown in for variety. Everything he could ask for.

The statuesque man beside Troy shifted, grounding his mind back into the present. Where it should have been in the first place.

Troy had been pulled from his turn as the school resource officer to escort the late-sixties man to Ross Witten's property recently inherited by his niece. Apparently, the Philadelphia Museum of Art contacted the Field Museum in Chicago this morning. They, in turn, ordered Richard Stanley to drop everything and spend three hours between airline and helicopter flights to reach Bell Edge as fast as possible.

Standing on Nicole Witten's doorstep, Troy couldn't stop obsessing about the reason for his presence. Nicole had unearthed buried treasure? Seriously? That was a real thing? And could the Chicago man's astonishing claim after that revelation honestly be true? Surely not. Movie and book plots didn't happen in real life. Yet, here he stood.

The front door flew open, and Troy forgot how to breathe.

Nicole was even more beautiful than the glimpse he'd caught of her picking up dinner days ago. According to the aging town matriarchs—who cornered him in the diner within minutes of Nicole's departure—she had spent summers in Bell Edge, but only occasionally visited the last few years, was thirty-one years old, and, most important of all, single. Looking at Nicole now, he'd swear she was in her early twenties. Max. Standing five foot five with black hair scraped into a ponytail, red, puffy eyes from crying, and—

Oh.

Her complexion turned whiter by the second.

He forgot he wasn't in his usual department-issued polo and khaki pants. Loosening his stance to soften his authoritative effect, he asked, "Nicole Witten?"

Gray eyes latched onto his, then slid down his pressed police uniform of dark gray, short-sleeved shirt, black pants, and leather utility belt holding the required gear. The full officer regalia tended to put people on edge, another reason, beyond comfort, he preferred his polo.

"Yes?" She met his gaze again, uncertainty and confusion seeping into her stance.

"Sorry for the intrusion," he offered to make up for the surprise ambush. "Can we come in?"

Her gaze flitted to Richard Stanley as she chewed on her lip, then with jerky motions signaled for them to follow her. Black athletic shorts, a stained pink T-shirt, and colorful cross-trainers stated she was tackling chores inside the house or about to continue her destruction of the landscaping.

Shutting the door behind himself, he trod from the foyer showcasing a quarter-turn staircase into the living room where chaos reigned.

Open packing boxes, piles ranging from linens to holiday items, and worn-out furniture crowded the room.

"Excuse the mess." Nicole scrubbed her hand over her face, a faint trembling revealing her nerves. "I'm in the middle of sorting through my uncle's stuff." She blinked rapidly, battling impending moisture. "And unpacking my own things."

"I'm sorry for your loss," Troy automatically responded, still taking in the disarray. Judging by the stacks of paperbacks and DVDs, she loved romance, comedies, thrillers, and epic sagas varying from *The Lord of the Rings*—extended editions—to the Marvel series.

A small catch of air had him peering up.

She lost the fight to the sheen filming her irises. A single tear slipped from the corner of her right eye. "I can't believe he's gone…" She lowered her head and sniffed.

Her sorrow ground against the grief constantly hounding Troy. The failure of his last case weighed on his soul, wrapping another layer of chains and constricting his ability to speak. All too well he understood Nicole's struggle to carry on with daily life while fighting not to drown.

"Sorry." Clearing her throat, she thrust her shoulders back, visibly marshaling her defenses. "What can I do for you?"

"I'm Richard Stanley." The suited gentleman held out a wrinkled hand.

Nicole shook it. "Nice to meet you, Mr. Stanley. And you

too, Officer—" she leaned forward to read the nameplate on his chest "—Hollenbeck."

"Detective," he corrected without thinking, so used to doing it. "But, please—" he rushed to smash the instant wall the formality created "—call me Troy."

"Oh. Um. Sure… Troy." A flush of pink stole over her skin, adding much-needed color to her still-white hue. "Can I offer you both some iced tea? I brewed it this morning."

"No need." Richard swished a hand. "I'd like to see the sword you've found."

Her mouth clamped shut and she blinked. A lot. "The sword? What? How did you know about that? It's only been about twenty-four hours since I dug it up. Who are you?"

Troy was about to respond, but Richard beat him to it.

"Forgive me for not introducing myself properly." Richard smoothed a liver-spotted hand down his conservative silk tie. "I'm an appraiser for the Field Museum in Chicago."

Nicole's pupils widened.

Troy's stomach tightened, knowing what was coming next.

Richard's stiff smile disappeared. "We believe the sword could be the one stolen from us twenty-five years ago."

Nicole gaped. "Did you say *stolen*?" She studied the aging man's face. Not a hint of teasing in his expression. "Wow. Um. Okay." She still hadn't processed the words. "Really?"

"Yes." Richard dipped his chin. "Really."

Surreal. Uncle Ross had a stolen sword on his property?

Nope. It didn't make sense. Her entire world hadn't made sense from the moment the attorney called to tell her about her uncle's passing. Now this? She couldn't wrap her head around the new information.

"How did you find out in Chicago?" Nicole asked again, stalling for time to absorb. "I mean, I contacted the Philadelphia Museum of Art *this morning*. They had me send pictures and said they'd get back to me."

She hadn't known what else to do. She wasn't versed in historical artifacts, and the item in the bundle had looked *old*. The only place she could think to start was the museum. She wasn't sure what she expected to happen next but it wasn't this bombshell.

"Yes, well." Richard brushed a piece of nonexistent lint off his expensive suit sleeve. "The museum community is small, and the theft is still discussed within our circles. A representative in Philadelphia contacted us. Your pictures match the stolen item, so I've been sent to examine the artifact."

With a police escort. Her eyes drifted to Detective Troy Hollenbeck. The honey-blond man could be featured in a calendar. Mr. February, in full uniform, holding a box of chocolates and a puppy. A slight whitening around the edges of his tanned face gave away he'd recently had a haircut. His clean-shaven jaw was rugged enough to be called masculine, and his bulletproof vest tried to hide his toned chest. He wasn't the tallest man she'd ever met, but the top of her head reached his beautiful blue eyes perfectly.

"A crate of five Viking artifacts loaned to us for an exhibition was stolen," Richard intoned. "The museum had to cancel the three-month-long event, losing a lot of money as well as integrity, which has taken years to overcome."

Five pieces were stolen? Her normally quick mind had trouble focusing. Weeks of endless grief weighed on her, and every task brought fresh bouts of memories, keeping her under.

Richard's gaze intensified. "Can you tell me how you found the Ulfberht?"

"The what?" Had she missed something? "Ulf…what?"

"Ulf…*beart*," Richard enunciated with a stuffy accent on the second syllable. "Ulfberht is the name of the master craftsman who forged the weapon."

"Oh." Duh. Yet, how would she know that?

"Only one hundred and seventy-one true Ulfberhts have been found so far."

"There were fakes?" Nicole leaned forward.

"Absolutely." Richard smiled like a man warming up for his favorite subject. "Just like we have counterfeit Rolexes and Gucci bags."

"Wow." Fascinating. "I never thought about someone knocking off a sword."

"The Ulfberht name carried a lot meaning." Richard's tone imparted his passion. "The production of the pure steel that made the sword strong, flexible, and lightweight had never been seen in Europe before and wouldn't be seen again for a thousand years."

Troy whistled.

"My sentiments exactly, Detective." Richard nodded. "Ms. Witten, I hate to push, but I'd really like to examine the sword."

"Oh." She straightened. "Of course. It's upstairs." She pivoted on her heel. "I'll be right back."

Curiosity gnawed. Was the artifact truly stolen? Could this all be a misunderstanding? Maybe she made a brand-new discovery. Had Vikings been in the Poconos way back then? Sadly, it embarrassed her to realize she didn't remember much from her ancient history lessons.

Just as she reached the quarter-turn platform of the steps, a floorboard overhead creaked.

She froze, her hand on the banister.

No one should be upstairs.

Chapter Three

Windows are open, Nicole's subconscious admonished. *Something fell over or tipped.*

Shaking her head at the sudden paranoia, she tackled the wooden steps. The faded and stained runner was another item on her long list to replace.

Reaching the top, a warm breeze brushed her skin, bringing the rich scent of the forest inside. The upstairs landing fed into a hallway that had two large bedrooms and a full bath on one side with the master suite and separate laundry room on the other.

Unable to touch the master bedroom, Nicole had claimed the farthest bedroom as her own. The second bedroom she used for storage and sorting. Maybe one day she'd be ready to tackle Uncle Ross's personal space, but not now.

Weathered cardboard boxes lined the hall, allowing just enough room for her to walk. Some had faded writing from Aunt Suzanne, while others had Nicole's scrawl to help the movers place them on the correct level. She was swimming in cardboard and started seeing the ugly brown in her dreams.

A door creaked behind her.

Slapping her hand on a scratched newel post, she whirled, her heart hammering her ribs.

She hadn't been in Uncle Ross's bedroom in days. That door had remained shut, but now it inched open.

"Hello?" she croaked, her voice catching thanks to the dryness overtaking her mouth.

"Ms. Witten?" Troy called from the bottom of the stairs.

She couldn't look away from the light steadily brightening the crowded hallway from a room that shouldn't be occupied.

A shadow began to form on the wooden floor, its shape growing progressively easier to identify.

Air sucked through her lips, and she had trouble swallowing.

"Nicole?" Troy called again. One heavy boot thumped on a step. "Do you need help with the sword?"

Sunlight streamed through the trees on the master side of the house, blinding her from details, but it didn't matter. The shadow took shape of a man looming in the doorway.

Blood roared through Nicole's veins. She stumbled backward, her heel slamming into a stack of boxes. They crashed into her legs, knocking her forward. Puzzle and game pieces dumped all over the floor.

"Nicole," Troy barked, his footsteps pounding the worn-out runner.

She scrambled to find footing in the mess.

"Where is it?" a deep male voice demanded, moving toward her.

A second set of shoes bombarded the staircase. "Ms. Witten?" Richard called.

"Tell me where it is," the stranger demanded again, the snarl raising the hair on her arms.

She couldn't move. Couldn't turn away. Couldn't take her eyes off the black gun aimed at her chest.

"Freeze," Troy shouted close behind her.

The stranger shifted his aim to her left. To Troy. "Drop it."

"Richard, stop," Troy ordered, seeming unfazed at the gun pointed at him.

The rumbling on the wooden steps ceased.

Black spots danced in Nicole's vision. She had to slow her breathing but couldn't control her body. Nothing worked in sync. Synapses fired different messages to her muscles: Run. Duck. Hide. Weep. Lose bladder control.

She fought hard against the last order.

"Put your hands up." Troy grazed her arm as he inched closer.

"Not another step, *Cop*."

Dear God, help.

The stairs creaked just as Richard exclaimed, "Jul—"

Gunfire ripped through the enclosed space, blasting her eardrums.

Nicole yelped, dropping low as she covered her head.

A second gunshot blasted, deafening everything.

She didn't think, just reacted. Pivoting on the balls of her feet, she scrabbled forward. Playing cards acted like ice taking her feet out from under her. She slammed to her hands and knees. Determined to get away, she ignored the biting pain digging into her skin. Puzzle pieces skittered ahead and fell through the railings. Finally finding a bit of traction, she crawled.

Movemovemovemove, she chanted, barreling over anything in her path.

A horrendous ringing continuously buzzed in her head, but she didn't care. She had to get away. Now.

Batting at a toppled box blocking her escape, she kept going.

Stay low, a voice coached in her mind. Worked for her. Reaching her bedroom door, she swatted the heavy wood moving in the breeze. The door bashed against the stopper and raced back toward her face.

Stop, her analytical side screamed. *You'll be trapped.*

No. She tipped over, smacking onto her butt as she tried to turn too fast.

You must hide, her terror ordered.

Glancing around wildly, she couldn't make up her mind. Flee or hide?

Her gaze landed on the opening for the stairs. Yes. Escape.

Scrambling to her hands and knees, she crawled forward,

ignoring the pain radiating from her abused kneecaps. More game pieces scattered and ricocheted off the baseboards. Another box in her way smacked against a wall. She finally reached the steps and froze.

"Richard," she cried. The once posh man lay crumpled on the steps. Unmoving. His eyes closed.

Large hands grabbed her shoulders.

"No," she screeched, flailing to break free. The stranger was not taking her anywhere.

The grip tightened and wrenched her backward. Her hands flew upward, punching anything in reach.

"Nicole," a sharp male voice barked.

"Let. Go." She continued the assault.

"Police."

Her fist froze mid-strike.

"Can you hear me?"

She blinked. Her ears still rang but not as loudly as before.

Two gorgeous blue eyes—the color of the Caribbean Sea—hovered above her.

Detective Troy Hollenbeck.

"You with me now?" he asked.

Fury, terror, pain, and shock swamped her at once.

She threw herself against his chest and burst into tears.

"Drink this." Troy set a black mug with the police department logo on the corner of a cluttered desk. "It's not gourmet, but it'll warm you up."

She hadn't stopped shaking since the guy with the gun—

A rush of air expelled from her mouth.

"Hey." Troy tucked a piece of her hair behind her ear. "You're okay."

She knew that on a cognitive level. Her body, on the other hand, hadn't gotten the message. The police had descended on her house like bees to a honeycomb. She had been chauffeured to the station downtown while the appraiser had been carted off in an ambulance.

Not her finest moment; Troy having to peel her off him with other officers watching. But she refused to be embarrassed—lie. She absolutely was but tried not to let it get to her. She was a dental hygienist for a reason. She didn't handle guns and blood well.

"Any word on Richard?" Nicole plucked the mug off the desk and wrapped her palms around the ceramic. The warmth felt good.

Troy marched to another desk in the open room and dragged a visitor's chair behind him. It bumped and hopped on the industrial carpeting. He set it in front of her and sat, his knees inches from hers. "Nothing yet."

The last she'd heard, the appraiser had taken a bullet somewhere in his chest. He had been alive when the paramedics arrived. She prayed he stayed that way.

The aroma of the steaming coffee was *strong*. Eye-popping, wouldn't-sleep-for-days strong. Best to not drink it. "I guess no one's caught the guy who broke in."

Troy shook his head, his eyes hardening. "We'll find him."

In the chaos, Nicole hadn't seen what happened, but Troy told her the gunman ran back into the master suite. He escaped over the balcony that ran the length of the house.

"Who's taking charge of this?" A female officer set a cardboard box onto a nearby desk.

The long-bottomed, four-inch-sided box looked like it had survived a war—or cheap movers in this case. Nicole had removed her belongings and placed the dirty bundle with the sword inside to keep it safe.

"Another appraiser's on the way," Officer Sam Dempsey answered, plopping into his office chair. He slapped a piece of paper on the desk. "Read over your statement, then sign at the bottom."

Nicole wasn't ready to relive the terrifying event just yet. Cradling the mug, she asked, "Do any of you know about the robbery?" She pointed at the box. "In Chicago?"

"I still can't believe you found this." The female officer motioned to the sword.

Sam sat back in the chair and rocked. "I did some digging after Troy left with Mr. Stanley to your house." He leaned forward and jabbed his keyboard. "Yeah, here it is." He pointed at the monitor.

Nicole tilted closer, but the angle wasn't the best for her to read. Not that her movement was wasted. She inhaled a healthy dose of Troy's soap or aftershave. The masculine clean scent helped settle her nerves.

"According to multiple newspaper stories, Salvatore Ricca, a.k.a. Sully, was suspected of ordering the theft but nothing was proven." Sam peered at Nicole. "Back then, he was the Boss of the Chicago Syndicate."

She shivered. The Syndicate was the longest-standing and most powerful organized crime organization in the city. News reports featured them way too often over the years. Unless a person lived under a rock, everyone knew about them.

"Drugs were, and still are, their main source of income, but they also had a hand in thefts of artifacts, jewelry, and intellectual property." Sam tapped his finger on the screen. "Quite a few articles allude to an employee of the Field Museum helping the thieves, but nothing's been proven."

Nicole sat back. "Did they arrest anybody?"

"Not that I could find. It's still unsolved." Sam tapped his mouse, scrolling down the page. He stopped and read, "'Sources close to the FBI state five crates containing Viking artifacts on loan from the National Museum of Denmark for an upcoming exhibit were stolen. Video security footage shows one of the thieves shooting two security guards during the escape while a third guard shot and killed a member of the heist crew.'"

Nicole set the untouched coffee on the desk. "Did the two security guards live?" Intuition told her they hadn't.

"No." Sam shook his head. "They died before paramedics arrived." He faced her. "Your uncle lived in Chicago at the time of the heist and now one of the stolen artifacts is potentially in that box." He jabbed a thumb at it. "Buried on your uncle's land."

She crossed her arms over her tightening chest. "Someone else could've put it there."

Troy's watchful expression grew grave. "We can't rule that out." He paused as if debating, then clapped his palms on his thighs. "No use speculating." Standing, he offered his hand. "I'll take you home."

Nicole allowed him to help her, but she couldn't stop the disappointment. He was going to say something important. She just knew it. What was he holding back?

Chapter Four

❧

Still raw, Nicole pushed the F-150's door on Troy's personal vehicle open, trying her best to ignore the implications from the police station. The puff of dirt from her tennis shoes landing wafted in the breeze. Her driveway had lost most of the gravel over the years. One day she'd have the long length paved.

Troy met her in front of the truck. Twice on the drive she'd almost asked him what he held back, but she chickened out. It was probably better she didn't know.

"You didn't have to get out." She swiped away strands of hair blowing against her mouth.

"Do you know that vehicle?" More aftershave or soap with a masculine scent drifted—

"Waffles!" a woman yelled from the direction of the Chevy pickup parked next to Nicole's Jeep. "Stop!"

"Ruff. Woof. Woof. Woof."

Air caught in Nicole's throat at the large black, brown, and white streak charging. Straight. At. Her.

"Waffles! Heel!" Wanda, Nicole's neighbor on the left, shouted.

Waffles kept running.

An iron grip clamped onto her forearm, yanking her sideways. Instantly off-balance, she fell against the back now blocking her view. Pushing against the bulletproof vest, she righted herself and took a step to the side. Troy mimicked her move to remain in the way.

Nicole shoved, but Troy only swayed.

"Stay behind me," he snapped, glaring over his shoulder.

Waffles darted around Troy, who tried his best to out-flank the dog but failed.

Heart lodged in her throat, Nicole grabbed the fabric of Troy's uniform with one fist and snapped up her other arm.

Waffles reared on two legs and slammed his front paws against her forearm. Seventy-plus pounds rammed against Nicole. She had no time to brace. Falling backward, she smashed into Troy, who tried to catch her, but they all landed in a heap.

"Woof. Woof. Woof." Bad doggy breath assailed her nose just as a pink tongue attacked her face. Nicole tried to block the wet bath, but Waffles was determined. Avid licks bombarded every available piece of skin.

"Waffles, stop that," Wanda scolded, panting at the same time.

Nicole cracked her eyelids, darting her chin away from another soaking. Standing above the pile was her pudgy, red-faced neighbor, sucking in air. Untamed gray curls surrounded a cherubic face, now scowling at the exuberant dog.

"Stop." Wanda grabbed onto the back of Waffles's harness and heaved. The dog resisted at first but relented when their rescuer snapped, "Heel."

Trembling with excitement, Waffles sat. His tail swished so hard his butt also pulsed. Floppy ears pricked upward as far as they could, bouncing with his two front paws alternately lifting while a long pink tongue hung out of one side of his panting mouth.

Wanda attached a leash onto the back of Waffles's harness.

Troy groaned.

"Oh!" Nicole scrambled upward. "Sorry." Mortification heated her cheeks. Why hadn't she already scooted off the detective?

"I think I broke my pride," Troy wheezed, rolling to one elbow before sitting up.

A bark of laughter erupted from Nicole's throat. She slapped a hand over her mouth but couldn't hold back the onslaught. The absurdity of the situation hit, and she couldn't hold it in. In one instant, her entire day turned around.

"Woof. Woof. Woof." Waffles stood, dancing in place as if laughing with her.

Troy slowly got to his feet, brushing at the dirt, missing more than he removed. "Well." He extended his neck left, then right, stretching the muscles. "It's hard to compete with that type of greeting."

"I'm so sorry." Wanda fiddled with a button on her tropical-themed shirt that matched her baggy crop pants. "He's fully trained. I promise."

Troy crouched and held out a hand for Waffles to sniff. Waffles lapped his palm instead. Troy laughed. The rich sound curled Nicole's toes.

"He was dropped off at the shelter three days ago." Wanda volunteered at the animal rescue four days a week. "After what happened today, Nicole, I thought you could use some protection."

Word spread fast in Bell Edge.

"Excellent idea." Troy ruffled Waffles's head.

Nicole wasn't sold but couldn't argue about having something with that many teeth keeping her safe.

Waffles preened under Troy's attention and rolled onto his back for tummy rubs.

"What type of dog is he?" Nicole had the room and time off work, but could she handle opening her heart so soon after losing her uncle?

Wanda smiled at the antics. "The former owner's daughter told us he's a little over a year old. He's a greater Swiss mountain dog and Labrador mix."

Waffles barked, sitting back up again.

"We dubbed him a Swissador." Wanda chuckled. "From my understanding, the seventy-six-year-old mother passed away. Every dog she rescued throughout her life was always named Waffles. The mother had trained the last Waffles to perform circus tricks and the one before that to be part of search and rescue."

Troy perked up. "Do you know what she trained this one to do?"

"Protection, for sure." Wanda shrugged. "The daughter mentioned police K-9 techniques."

That could mean anything. Nicole chewed on her lip. Did he sniff out drugs? Explosives? Missing socks? Either way, it sounded like he'd be great against intruders.

A soft woof emanated as the dog pranced toward Nicole. She knelt, one knee grinding into the dirt. Waffles stopped in front her, his height having them practically eye to eye. Tail still wagging, he locked his brown eyes with hers. Nicole realized there was no decision.

Throwing her arms around the goofball, a fresh puff of dirt coated her tongue. "We're going to rescue each other, big guy."

Chapter Five

Julien Renaud finagled the smaller rental RV onto the lumpy ground beside the dirt access road and turned the engine off.

The entire area plunged into darkness without his headlights. He shivered, spooked at the complete absence of light. Thanks to the thick forest canopy and clouds, no stars or moon illuminated the night sky. Who in their right mind wanted to live in a horror movie setting?

He needed Chicago's man-made illumination and noise pollution.

Dropping onto the bench seat behind the built-in table, he snapped on a lamp near the curtained window. Nothing had gone as planned today.

If he'd had more time and notice, he could've come up with a better plan to steal the sword. He'd left the moment he saw the email from the Philadelphia Museum of Art in the general in-box, but it wasn't soon enough. He arrived minutes after Richard and the cop. They should've been a great distraction. He'd slip in, take the sword, and leave unnoticed, but that hadn't worked. Richard loved artifacts and mysteries, and he pressed to see the sword before Julien could find it.

Julien just hoped he silenced the man soon enough. He needed more time, and it went without saying, he never wanted the cops to learn of his involvement.

They were both appraisers for the Field Museum. They'd crossed paths many times over the years but weren't buddies. Julien wasn't friends with anyone at the museum for a reason. He'd worked hard to follow in his father's footsteps. He graduated top of his class at Loyola, obtained an appraiser certification, and became a consultant with the Field Museum, all so he could spy for the Chicago Syndicate and listen for any signs of the stolen Viking treasure.

The very treasure his father, Emile Renaud, helped steal all those years ago. Then, it disappeared. No one in The Syndicate could figure out who stole it from them after the museum heist and how. Now, whispers on the black market of at least four of the Viking artifacts surfacing raged. The seller remained as much a mystery as the buyers, but after today, Julien suspected Ross Witten was behind the sales. The former lawyer used to fence all the "procured" items for The Syndicate and had been against the Viking heist from the beginning.

Squeezing his clenched fists, Julien growled. That traitor swore he didn't know who took the treasure after Julien's father had secured it in The Syndicate's warehouse. Liar.

Emile Renaud *died* searching for those stupid artifacts. It was only fair that Julien meted the same justice to the Wittens. Ross's heart attack robbed Julien of the satisfaction of making the traitor pay, but all was not lost. Nicole worked nicely to take the former lawyer's place.

After she solved the riddle.

He snatched the document he'd stolen out of the file on Ross's dresser. Spreading the trifold flat, he stared at three stanzas on the white page.

The first sentence gave coordinates to start the search, then the riddle itself separated into three stanzas, then, closed with a message to combine the answers to find the treasure.

Julien deserved that treasure and more. And Nicole was going to give him everything.

He'd already scoped the designated area and found a brand-new retreat center under construction. With a little digging on a few paid internet sites, Julien learned that Ross owned the property and development for an expensive haven. Financing details were sparse to nonexistent, but the estimate was in the millions. No doubt it was the traitor's way of laundering the money from the stolen artifact sales. He used to advise Salvatore Ricca to use real estate as one of the avenues to obscure revenue streams.

Now it was Julien's turn to reap the benefits. Nicole was going to sign over everything Ross owned before she died. To accomplish everything, he had to lure her on-site.

He'd already put part of his plan into action. By impersonating George Hearn, a real County Planning and Development Division employee, Julien halted the retreat center's construction for the next few days. With no one on the premises, he had room to work without witnesses.

The second stage of his plan began tomorrow morning. Good ole fake George was going to call Nicole and talk her into visiting the site.

Julien's eyes strayed to the long, hard case resting on the other side of the seating. He had walked the location earlier, after the workers went home, and found the perfect place to set up his sniper rifle. As much as he wanted to use the weapon on Ross's only living relative, he'd restrain himself. He'd make do with taking out her vehicle.

With her far from safety and help, he'd have all the time in the world to exact his revenge.

Chapter Six

Parking behind a black Suburban blocking in Nicole's Jeep, Troy exited his personal truck. Men and women in the vicinity wearing evidence collection coveralls took note of his presence, then went back to work. Since he had on his comfortable khaki cargo shorts and Phillies T-shirt, he doubted any of them knew he worked for BEPD. As it was his day off, he wanted to keep it that way as long as possible.

"Look at this."

He snapped his attention to the beautiful five-foot-five woman vibrating with fury. The big Suburban had hidden Nicole initially. Waffles trotted by her side on a leash attached to his harness.

The dog reared up and slapped his big front paws on Troy's chest.

"How's my main man?" Troy scratched the Swissador. "Did you protect your mom last night?" Troy had slept better knowing she had the dog.

"Ruff. Woofwoofwoof."

She waved a folded sheaf of papers. "The FBI handed me this search warrant."

He wasn't surprised. If he'd led the investigation, he'd have done the same thing. "You have to—"

"They're allowed to comb through every inch of my house as well as the grounds."

The quaver at the end made him pay attention. She was angry, understandably, but her gray irises also hinted at fear. And no wonder. A ton of federal agents had descended on her house.

"They woke me up." She shoved the papers into a side pocket on her athletic shorts. "I'm not allowed to touch *anything*. I haven't even had my coffee yet."

Oh, boy. Processing all this on no caffeine…cruel.

"I can fix that." He opened his passenger door. "We'll hit the diner in town—"

"What is that?" She pointed at the huge bag of dried dog food on the seat.

His cheeks warmed. "I, uh, thought you could use it." He rubbed the back of his neck. "I have the day off and, um, thought the three of us could go shopping. For Waffles."

He sounded like a teenager asking a girl out for the first time. The grief weighing on his soul eased around her, and he didn't know how to handle that. He never factored in meeting anyone when he left Philadelphia. All he wanted was to find a way to keep putting one foot in front of the other until it didn't hurt so much anymore. But something deep inside him called for her. Which was mighty inconvenient. He had barely settled in Bell Edge and carried seeping baggage from his last case.

"I, uh—" he cleared his throat "—may have already scoped the mega pet store about a half hour from here."

Nicole's lips parted into a gorgeous smile. "This guy—" she scratched Waffles's head "—conned me out of half of my dinner and tried to sleep in the bed last night. I need *a lot* of stuff." She bit her lip. "But I can't. I, um, have somewhere I need to be." She gazed toward her Jeep. "I don't know if the lead FBI guy—"

"I'll drive you." Troy hauled out the *heavy* bag of food. Nicole opened the second passenger door—the four doors allowed him to cart extra people as well as stuff. He dropped the dog food on the rubber floor mat.

"I can't ask you to do that."

"You didn't." Troy motioned for her to hop in. "I offered."

"It's kinda far."

Waffles jumped onto the cushioned bench in the back, showing his vote.

"No problem. You can't do anything here anyway."

"True." Nicole used the step-rail and handlebar to climb into the passenger seat.

Once Troy settled behind the wheel and had them traversing the driveway, he asked, "Where we headed?"

"Outside Long Barn." She named a small township about an hour north, deeper in the mountains. In fact, he grew up an hour west of Long Barn before he moved to Philadelphia. His parents still lived in the same house.

"George Hearn," she continued, "from the county's Planning and Development Division called this morning."

He hadn't expected that response. "Why?"

"Apparently—" she fidgeted with the hem of her T-shirt "—my uncle's developing a retreat center. It's currently under construction. There are some environmental and structural issues I have to deal with."

"What?" The question was out before he stopped the stupid response.

"Yeah." The hem rolled and unrolled in her fingers. "His will never mentioned anything about the property or development." She pushed the button to slide Waffles's window down. The dog shoved his big head outside. "Two point six million dollars."

"What?" Troy idiotically asked again. He needed to expand his vocabulary.

"That's how much Uncle Ross has spent, according to the county guy."

Troy whistled.

"I've never had the impression my uncle was rich, yet…" She scrubbed her face. "This is all so unbelievable," she muttered. "Stinson, the lead FBI agent, had no problem letting me know he didn't like Ross." Her sudden topic change showcased her inner turmoil. "He had just been assigned to the Chicago office when the heist happened and said Uncle Ross had only one client."

Troy tightened his grip. Richard Stanley had let the name slip on their ride to Nicole's house. Troy almost told her at the station but hadn't wanted to pass on unconfirmed information.

"Uncle Ross *wouldn't* represent Salvatore Ricca." Her hands balled into fists. "He wasn't unscrupulous or shady." Her voice caught. "He taught me right from wrong and hammered home strong moral values. Does that sound like a criminal to you?" She jabbed a finger toward Troy. "He had a robust laugh and considered everyone a friend. Everyone loved him."

Especially you, Troy mentally added, her grief and disbelief rubbing against his own despair living below the surface.

Waffles shoved his head between the seats and licked Nicole's cheek, then nudged his snout against Troy's bicep.

"The FBI investigated my uncle twenty-five years ago in connection to the heist." She snorted. "*Of course* they didn't find anything. He's *innocent*."

Not finding something was a far cry from being innocent. Troy met her tormented gaze, then focused back on the winding, two-lane road. Did she want him to interject or listen?

"According to this—" she swiped a hand at the warrant now on the console, flapping in the wind "—they're searching for more stolen items and evidence the other artifacts were on the property."

Waffles whined, resting his head on her shoulder.

"*Were* on the property?" Troy repeated. "Are you saying they found the rest of the Viking artifacts?" Since yesterday? How had he not heard anything about the discoveries?

"No. Yes," Nicole growled. "Two agents were talking about rumors their team were trying to validate. Something about the other stolen pieces recently sold on the black market."

And Nicole was headed to an undisclosed retreat center under construction that had received a substantial amount of money from Ross Witten.

Recent artifact sales. New construction.

Red flags flapped hard in Troy's mind. Pieces of the puzzle were starting to come together, and it wasn't looking good for Ross.

Was the retreat center a legitimate investment or a way to launder money? The will not reflecting ownership or disclosing how he expected to recoup his money could be as innocent as Ross dying before he contacted the lawyer… or purposefully hiding the connection.

How did the County Planning and Development Division know to call Nicole? Something didn't add up, and that set him on edge.

He couldn't fail again. During his last investigation in Philadelphia, a mother and child were executed because they had witnessed a murder. Troy's job had been to catch the killer but he hadn't been quick enough and the mother and child paid the price. On top of that, his partner had been shot multiple times when they had attempted to arrest the suspect. Thanks to Troy's inadequacy, his partner had medically retired from a job he loved.

And now, Nicole had been threatened at gunpoint, Richard fought for his life, and a potential money-laundering scheme loomed on the horizon. All surfaced because of an unearthed buried treasure linked to a museum heist twenty-five years ago.

He *had* to succeed this time.

One failure was one too many, and his partner owned that one. Richard claimed the second when Troy didn't secure the house before the meeting. Sloppy police work. He refused to add a third to the list.

Did the FBI know about the retreat center and the county employee's phone call? He'd bet his next paycheck Nicole hadn't said a word. Her rant would've included a team of agents peeling off to investigate the place. That lead FBI agent didn't do himself any favors by alienating Nicole. She obviously had no problem letting Troy— a BEPD detective—know about the latest development.

That left *him* to report the new information.

He snuck a peek at his and Nicole's cellphones charging. Neither showed a signal. Great. They weren't far from their destination. Hopefully he'd pick up a bar or two there.

Chapter Seven

Resting his hands on his hips, Troy scanned the immediate area. Dry dirt from his trek up the steep grade drifted in a breeze. At one point, he thought he'd have to switch to four-wheel drive. Deep ruts, sharp turns, and the arduous angle challenged his aging F-150.

Ross had chosen a beautiful, forested, and remote location. They had driven through Long Barn, then continued on the paved two-lane road for another sixteen miles.

Sunlight dappled overgrown vegetation and full-grown trees as it filtered through the canopy. Sections of the forest had been cleared for construction. To his left, a large building loomed, composed of wooden slats, beautiful stone on the lower half, and oversize windows. The exterior seemed finished, but the partially open main doorway revealed stacks of lumber, machinery, and unfinished floors inside.

Scattered outside, heavy equipment such as an excavator and backhoe sat forlornly, their operators missing.

In fact, everyone was missing. It wasn't Sunday, so where was the construction crew?

The hair on the back of his neck rose. Silence. Too much silence laded the air. Birds didn't warble. Insects didn't buzz. Squirrels weren't clambering on the trees.

Nicole stopped beside Troy. "Is it just me or does it feel creepy?"

"Grrrrrrrrrr. Wooooof." Waffles's scruff lifted. His brown eyes locked onto something beyond a large tractor loader and trees on the right. Lowering his head, he growled. Menace poured off the dog. *"Woofwoofwoofwoofwoof."*

Troy yanked up the back of his T-shirt and snatched his personal 9 mm Berretta from its holster. He'd donned the weapon before exiting the truck. Wild animals were a fact of life in the mountains. A shotgun was better, but he'd make do with the handgun. Unless it was a bear. His Berretta would only make it mad.

"Troy?" Nicole whispered, clutching the base of her throat.

The tremulous question ratcheted his anxiety. Flashbacks of his former partner jolting as bullets slammed into his body tried to take hold. Troy forcefully pushed them aside. He couldn't...*wouldn't* fail again.

"Behind me," he ordered, straining to see whatever caught Waffles's attention.

A muted crack echoed just as his right front tire rocked.

Troy whirled, grabbing Nicole, dragging her to the other side of the truck. A bullet couldn't penetrate the engine block.

"Not again," Nicole yelped.

Waffles barked, fighting the sudden new direction.

The truck shimmied just as another muted shot echoed in the breeze.

"Sniper rifle with a suppressor," Troy announced for no other reason than to channel his racing thoughts. Shotguns were loud and fired cartridges full of pellets. But a typical sniper rifle had a suppressor dampening the sound and discharged bullets, giving the shooter an advantage and lethal accuracy. "He's shooting out my tires."

"Your tires?" Nicole squawked, stopping mid-crouch. "He'll get us then." She pointed at the wheel in front of their faces.

"Only if he moves." Troy risked a peek around the front bumper. "He's not at the right angle."

High-pitched shattering snapped him backward. The

F-150's windshield and passenger door window crackled from bullet holes.

"Dear God." Nicole hugged Waffles closer, but the dog squirmed to break free.

Helpless rage tore through Troy.

More bullets slammed into the truck.

He threw his body over Nicole and Waffles.

The glass lost against the onslaught, bursting inside with some raining down on them. By the sounds, his dashboard and everything else in the gunman's scope splintered.

Nicole shook so hard, Troy had to squeeze tighter to maintain his hold. His ears rang from Waffles's barking and the bullets' destruction.

At a pause, Troy let go. Resituating his Beretta, he peered around the front bumper again.

Waffles growled, his head beside Troy's hip. Nicole had a white-knuckled grip on the leash, holding him back.

"Ummm, Detective." Her soft words quavered. "Shouldn't you be calling nine-one-one? The FBI? Marines?"

A new barrage of bullets drove him behind the tire. "Phone's in the truck."

God, Troy silently spat, not having much faith anymore. *How could You put Nicole in jeopardy?* He was so tired of evil constantly winning.

"Oh, man," Nicole hissed. "Mine, too."

Sudden silence thundered louder than the assault.

He risked another look. Leaves danced in a gentle breeze, and the sun still blazed. No wayward shadows or hint of the sniper revealed.

He counted ten seconds.

Nothing.

"We gotta move." Troy calculated the distance between the truck and the looming main building. *One hundred yards give or take.* He bit back choice words. A lot of open ground once they left the safety of the truck.

"Won't he shoot us?" Nicole stroked the dog like her life depended on it.

"If he's had any kind of training—" Troy hunched, keeping his Beretta pointed at the ground "—he'll shift to keep me from locking in on him."

A sickly shade of ash replaced vitality. "Oh." She lifted her butt, mimicking his stance. "Right."

"Head for that open door." Troy pointed. Her pupils were so large he wasn't sure how much she processed. "Run as fast as you can. Once you get inside, stay below the windows. He can't shoot through stone."

The last bit of color drained from her face.

"Run," Troy snapped to reach through the shock. "Now."

Chapter Eight

"God, help. God, help," Nicole prayed over and over, bolting for the entrance.

Waffles ran beside her.

Adrenaline practically gave her feet wings. Any second she expected a bullet to slam into her back. To keep from losing her mind, she purposefully focused on the details in front of her.

The inviting front porch had three wide steps plus an accessible ramp. It ran the length of the structure and was deep enough to support a swing.

Her athletic shoes slapped against the ramp, pounding the wood into submission. Waffles's nails clicked with his strides. She slammed into the wood-and-glass door, pushing it out of the way.

Bounding to the left, she dropped below the windows. Air seemed in short supply and gasping didn't help, just added blackness to her vision.

Waffles licked her bruised knees from yesterday's crawling plight. He put his nose on the dusty cement foundation floor and snuffled the length of his leash.

"Come here." She heaved, terrified the shooter would see the dog and…and… She swallowed around the lump clogging her throat. She couldn't lose Waffles.

Bang.

She jumped, the back of her hand smacking an unfinished electrical socket. Her bladder threatened to loosen. Whipping her gaze up, she found Troy hunch-jogging toward her after shutting the door.

Relief, horror, and terror spurred the tears crowding her eyes. Try as she might, she couldn't stop shaking.

"You did awesome." Hard shards in his blue eyes softened. "I think you broke a land speed record."

"Usain Bolt. That's me." She sniffed hard and clamped a shaking hand over the other.

The right side of his lips quirked "We can't stay here." His gaze roved the interior.

Fear urged her to leap to the next hiding place while at the same time cementing her shoes to the floor. Scraping her cheeks against her T-shirt sleeves, she smeared the waterworks refusing to quit. Thankfully she hadn't worn makeup since she moved to Bell Edge. Runny mascara would add a cherry to this nightmare.

"Follow me."

Her eyes latched onto his. Determination stared back. *Detective* Troy Hollenbeck was now in charge. The maelstrom inside quieted, allowing her to take a full breath.

"Stay as low as you can and pay attention to Waffles."

She nodded automatically, then absorbed the instructions. "Wait. Why pay attention to Waffles?"

Troy sunk into his crouch. "His senses are better than ours."

Oh. Duh. "Got it." Now. But for an idiotic second she thought Troy meant the dog would misbehave.

Troy rose slightly and hustled forward. The cavernous space had cathedral ceilings and a massive stone fireplace and would probably become the main lounge when finished. For now, stacks of lumber sprawled among various machinery and toolboxes.

She loosened the hold on Waffles's leash and allowed him to trot in front of her. The dog stuck to Troy's heels.

The detective rushed through a doorless opening.

Nicole's back protested the awkward position, but she wouldn't stand until he did. The next empty room was almost as large as the last, though it had a full wall of windows on the one side, from knee height to a few feet from the ceiling.

Waffles snuffled as Troy ran upright for a doorway on the right side.

Nicole followed suit. The windows gave her the creeps. The sight beyond may be beautiful, but the room was too open. Anyone could see in.

She dashed into an industrial kitchen.

Waffles growled, then bolted forward, yanking her wrist. Hard. She smacked into the end of a long stainless steel island. That didn't deter the dog. He kept dragging her forward.

Troy pivoted near a gleaming, eight-burner stove, his attention riveted on Waffles. "Whatcha sense, big guy?"

The dog's ear twitched, but he otherwise kept pulling.

Nicole jumped over a haphazard pile of metal rails with hooks on the tile floor. The pans they would ultimately hang were still packed inside boxes stashed by the washing sinks.

Ahead, next to a closed exterior door, clear, plastic gallon jugs sat on the bottom of wire shelving. "What are those?"

"Waffles, stop." Troy's boot steps vibrated the metal rails, toppling a few over.

The dog froze, one paw in the air. Lifting his head, he peered at Troy marching past.

Troy crouched, his gun dangling between his knees. He studied the single-line, P-Touch labels on each. "I have a clue the direction of Waffles's training." He swiped the sweat dotting his forehead. "They're all full of potassium chlorate."

"What's that?" The foreboding building inside Nicole threatened to take over.

"Depends on who's using it." Troy twisted, his expression grim. "It's easy to make and used as a disinfectant *or* a component in a bomb."

Chapter Nine

Troy surged upward. "We need to move."

"Woof." Waffles bounded to Troy's side.

Nicole's pasty skin flushed. "Where?"

Good question. He had no clue. The shooter could be anywhere, and without blueprints, Troy didn't know the layout of the site.

"Outside." But he needed a different exit. Training kicked in, not allowing him to use the same egress twice. The enemy had had time to set a trap, and Troy wasn't running into it.

Dodging around the steel island secured to the floor, he raced back into the immense empty room. The wall of windows heightened his nerves. The three of them were like fish in a bowl. A bullet could easily find them with nothing to use as cover.

Nails clicking and shoes slapping told him Nicole and Waffles were right behind him. He exhaled. Keeping them safe was his main priority. Leaving the building was a risk, but staying inside had them trapped. Using the forest terrain and whatever structures existed gave them options.

Two single-wide glass doors spaced twenty feet apart on the other side of the room led to a large open deck. He slowed and pushed on a thin, horizontal bar. The door swung easily.

He held it for Nicole and the dog. "Kneel next to the benches." Built-in seating with solid backs lined the outer section of the deck.

Doubt assaulted him. He could be making a huge mistake. Nicole's and Waffles's lives literally depended on his decisions. The responsibility tried to crush him, but he couldn't let it. Failure was not an option. Cliché but too true.

Nicole huddled, one bloodless hand fumbling to free the leash from her red-raw wrist. Running to her position, he longed to soothe the sore skin but didn't dare. At any moment, he might have to fight or use the Beretta to save her life. She mattered more than his need for a connection and comfort.

Raising his head just high enough, he surveyed the immediate area. Trees and vegetation had been cleared for at least two hundred feet. Dry dirt, construction detritus, and a full dumpster littered the ground. Leaves shushed in the constant breeze, but nothing else stirred. Idyllic if it weren't for the gun-wielding psycho.

Where was the county employee, George Hearn? Had he been a victim of a sniper bullet? Or was he part of whatever was going on?

A more pressing question: Did Troy lead or follow? Which direction had the most threat? In front or behind?

No answer struck him. Of course not. God hadn't been helpful in a long time. Troy had seen and experienced too much of humanity's worst to have much faith. He might have gotten beyond that if his partner hadn't been shot. His tenuous thread with God snapped. He no longer listened to lectures about God's benevolence or how everything was part of God's plan. A criminal killed a mother and daughter, then permanently injured a good man attempting to bring the dirtbag to justice. God should've been looking out for that family and his partner. They were on the right side of the law.

Just as Nicole and Richard were innocents who should have God's protection.

Waffles flattened to his belly, trying to poke his nose through the one-inch gap between the deck and bench bottom.

A light bulb clicked in Troy's brain. He had a resource he didn't have on his last case in Philadelphia.

The dog. Waffles wasn't a full-fledged police K-9, but his innate senses far surpassed Troy's.

A large snort emanated. Waffles jolted to his paws and whirled, taking off before Troy could process the intent.

"Waffles," Nicole hissed, lunging to grab the trailing leash. She missed. The front of her body smacked onto the deck.

Troy tried to catch her but was too late. He cuffed her ribs and gouged the wood with the Beretta in his attempt.

She thrust upward, striking his jaw with her head. But the hit didn't slow her scramble after Waffles.

Troy rushed to his feet, rubbing his throbbing chin, and managed to avoid another strike by centimeters.

The wood vibrated beneath seventy-plus pounds as Waffles charged for the opening in the wooden seating and railing.

"Waffles," Nicole hissed again, hot on the canine's trail. "Stop."

The dog stuttered, then took off.

Troy hurtled after the two, overhearing snatches of Nicole's fierce muttering: "...*not* fully trained..."

"...sign you up...obedience..."

"...no treats for life."

Troy agreed. He knew a handler for military K-9s. He should enroll Waffles. Bet the dog wouldn't disobey a command again once he graduated.

Pounding down two steps, dirt puffed beneath his boots, mixing with the trail left behind by Nicole and Waffles. Adrenaline pumping, his head swiveled as he tried to take in everything. Their running was the opposite of stealth. The shooter only needed to listen to zero in on their location. Nicole's focus was on catching the dog. Whether she realized it or not, she trusted Troy to pay attention to everything else. To warn her if an immediate threat materialized.

He wasn't worthy of the trust, but he'd do his best anyway.

Waffles hurtled toward the forest, leaping and dodging everything in his path.

Troy winced. The leash barely missed catching on a metal tooth of a backhoe. The eight-foot nylon length either had to come off or they had to do a better job containing the dog's impulses. He couldn't live with himself if something happened to Waffles. Or Nicole. The terror of those thoughts almost had him praying again. Almost.

The temperature dropped when he plunged into the tree shade. Silence still pervaded. The only sounds came from their harsh breathing and footsteps resembling a fleeing herd of hippos.

Creepy didn't begin to describe the utter stillness. The animals and insects had vanished or did an awesome job of burrowing. Something he, Nicole, and Waffles should be doing.

If he ever found a spot safe enough.

The terrain began to swiftly angle upward on the left, making running awkward. Massive boulders jutted from the ground sporadically, covered in moss and forest debris. Virginia creeper vines snagged around his ankles, tripping him every other step. Mountain maple bushes smacked into his legs, and he hoped with all his might poison ivy wasn't entangled within. Itchy rashes were the last thing he needed.

Waffles immerged into a smaller clearing. The plants hadn't been emptied as thoroughly as the main building's area. Gashes marred the inclined land where an excavator dug in to level a swath large enough for the partially constructed cabin. The single-story structure had the makings of a lavish getaway.

Waffles disappeared inside.

Nicole plunged in after the dog with no hesitation.

Troy's heart stuttered. *Please, don't let the sniper be hiding in there.* He leaped through the doorway, snapping his gun up. Something attracted Waffles. The gunman? The county employee? More explosive components? Too many unknowns, and Nicole dismissed them all to capture the dog.

His blond hair was going to turn white soon.

Two-by-fours spaced sixteen inches apart framed out rooms. No drywall had been attached yet, allowing him to see almost the entire space. Left, right, front, behind, he searched for a threat. Nothing. Just Nicole still chasing Waffles.

Unlike the main building, this cabin had no cement foundation. Footsteps rang hollow, revealing a gap between the ground and the plywood flooring. Waffles shot through the two-by-fours effortlessly. Nicole twisted sideways to fit.

"Woof." Waffles darted toward the back corner of the cabin. In less than a second, Troy lost visual of the dog. Tall sections of heavy granite countertops, unattached doors, multi-gallon containers, lumber, toolboxes, and so much more cluttered that area.

Thwump. Something fell, shaking the whole cabin.

"No," Nicole yelled, disappearing. "Waffles, heel. Stop!"

Troy dashed through the maze of doorways, not trusting he'd fit between the gapped studs.

A piercing canine yelp chilled his blood.

"Waffles," Nicole shrieked.

On the verge of hulking through the framing, Troy finally found the doorway leading to the corner. His stomach plunged as black spots swarmed his vision.

"No!" he shouted, diving forward. Half of Nicole's body disappeared into a large, jagged hole in the floor. He threw his arms around her calves, drilling his knees into the ply-wood for traction.

Hair-raising cracking echoed. Before he could take a breath, the wood gave way beneath him.

Chapter Ten

Nicole couldn't breathe. Couldn't scream. Couldn't do anything but drop. Headfirst.

Black nothingness terrified her to the point of incapacity.

She had no time to think beyond: *I'm going to break my neck.*

Something heavy crashed into her, then wrapped itself around her body from behind. It lifted her top half, yanking her sideways—

Wham. She slammed into the bottom of the hole.

Every muscle, bone, and cell jarred, clacking her teeth painfully.

Rattled, she didn't realize she was rolling until a wave of dizziness swamped her muddled brain.

"Oomph," a voice wheezed next to her ear just as they stopped moving.

A cacophony of crashes deafened.

Stale air coated with particles smacked her face and body.

"Ruff. Woof. Woof."

"Waffles." Nicole couldn't see anything in the pitch-dark. "Are you okay, big guy?"

Slobbery wetness coated her cheek, forehead, neck, and every available surface of skin.

The licking ceased, but she sensed the dog over the top of her head.

"Thanks for the bath," a voice croaked.

"Troy?" Her mind still swam in her skull.

"Yeah?" Something shifted behind her. "Ooooohhhh. That hurts."

It took too many seconds for her to connect the dots, then she understood. Troy had fallen in, wrapped around her, then rolled them out of the way of whatever fell in next.

"Are you hurt?" Troy asked. A heaviness disappeared from her ribs, and she figured it was his arm.

The tags on Waffles's collar jingled. Either the dog shook himself or Troy scratched the area.

Another weight lifted, freeing her legs. "Can you... Something's digging into my back."

Nicole winced. Rattled brain or not, she should have moved right away. "Sorr—owwwwwwwwwww." Flattening on her back after rolling forward, she panted, breathing through the agony.

"Nicole?" Worry laced Troy's tone as a scraping echoed.

"I'm okay," she lied through gritted teeth. Every cell she owned burned and screamed. "I'm pretty sure nothing's broken." Once she had the energy, she'd pat herself down, but until then, she'd wheeze and suffer in silence. "What about you?"

"I'll live," he answered, then muttered under his breath, "I think."

Cool, dank air set into her bones, adding a lovely layer of ache. She couldn't pin down the smell, but earthy mossy staleness surrounded her...

Then it truly set in. She couldn't. See. A. Thing. Like seriously couldn't see *any*thing. She'd always hated the dark ever since she was little. Her overactive imagination kicked in and fried logic. Every. Time. It didn't matter how often her mom or Uncle Ross checked her room, she had to have a night-light.

"Am I blind," she whispered, "or is there no light?"

"No light."

No. No. No. Sweat tickled her forehead. *You're fine. You just need a distraction.* "That was some heroics, Detective Hollenbeck. Did they teach that maneuver in the police academy?" she snarked, attempting to divert her mind. "What was the class called? How to Surf a Civilian?" Images of uniformed men and women practicing lightened the oppression, then reality crashed back in. "Why did someone shoot at us? Is it the same guy, or am I just that unpopular?"

"Hey."

She jumped at the soft voice mere inches from her face. She hadn't heard him move, but then, her nerves were redlining.

Her hair shifted. Had he petted her?

"You're—"

"You smell good," she blurted, ignoring the construction dust and underground dank. "*Er...* Um." Her distraction apparently wanted to become a confession. "I mean... I know you bathe and stuff. Maybe even do that guy thing where you use one bottle for your hair and skin." *That's enough, Distraction.* "Not that I'm snorting you like candy." She totally was.

Waffles's collar jingled again.

She couldn't pinpoint the dog's location.

The weight of the darkness closed in.

Okay, Distraction, let 'er rip. "I'm going to just put this out there, Detective." Not seeing his face made her much braver than normal. "You're pretty. I mean handsome."

A catch of air close to her ear.

"You've got this appealing magnetism, but something haunts you—"

She hadn't meant to say that.

"Don't stop there." Laughter tinged the words. "I gotta hear the rest."

"Nah. I said enough." A little too much.

"Way to end on a cliffhanger," he teased.

She melted. He hadn't made fun of her or prodded to hear more. Just like he hadn't ridiculed or treated her like a weak female after she cried in his arms in the aftermath of violence in her home.

Warning. Warning. Her heart barely handled accepting Waffles. The grief ruling the organ drained her dry. But bigger than that, her judgment was in question. She didn't want to believe anything the FBI said about Uncle Ross, but she couldn't outright ignore it either. A part of her now asked: Who was Uncle Ross really? A devoted and loving man raising her with strong morals, or a savvy criminal, eluding authorities all these years?

Enough. "I'm sitting up." Slowly using her abdominal muscles, she clenched her jaw at jostling her aching bones. A warm hand braced her back and she flinched, wanting the strength, but cautious of it.

A furry body wiggled next to her other side, then bad breath blasted her face.

"Troy?" She hated the wobble in her voice. "Can we get out of here?"

Chapter Eleven

Every throbbing muscle Troy owned froze at the question. His pounding headache stalled, and his twinging back stilled. She needed him to say yes. But he wouldn't lie.

"I don't know." He steeled himself to find out if they were buried alive.

The underground temperature hovered in the sixties, and a damp mustiness invaded his nose, threatening long bouts of sneezing. Just what he needed on top of everything else.

"Nicole," he rasped, "do you feel a wall or anything next to you?"

He already calculated there was about two feet on their right from his trek to her.

"Waffles, move." Clothing shifted and the dog stopped panting. "Yes. It's smooth and soft. Packed dirt maybe?"

So, they were in approximately a five-foot-wide space. Now, how tall was it? Could they climb out the way they came in?

"I lost my scrunchie." Air shifted with her mysterious movements. "My hair's going to get in the way… Not important. Never mind."

An image of her long black hair flowing around her face arrested him. He wanted to see that in real life, not his imagination.

Rein it in. Concentrate on the priority.

Holding his breath, he planted a hand on the ground and pushed. So much pain exploded everywhere, he sucked in a breath. Dizziness tilted him backward. Pushing through it, he balanced over his boots. Raising an arm above his head, he lifted his butt, hunching. Open space continued above him. Straightening slowly, he wasn't surprised he could stand upright. The fall had seemed forever. Above, his fingertips met something rough and long, spanning sideways. Timber? Bracing of some kind? Either way, the height was over six feet—

Wait. He lowered his right arm and flexed his fingers open and closed. His Beretta was gone. When the floor cracked, his only thought had been to clear Nicole out of the way of debris falling in after them. Short-term importance, long-term stupidity.

His empty hand curled into a fist in disgust. Nicole relied on him to keep her alive, and he couldn't manage his weapon. She deserved better than him.

He had a tactical knife clipped to his waist, but it didn't do anything against bullets.

Fingernails bit into his palms. God had abandoned Nicole. Just like He'd deserted Troy months ago. Troy could rail and rage, but it wouldn't change a thing. They had to rely on themselves to stay alive.

So stop grinding your teeth and get to it. Using his sense of touch, he explored overhead. Another thick timber stretched across, then…rock? Something cold and coarse. He kept going. *Ouch.* Sharp, splintery edges dug into his skin. Pieces of the jagged plywood flooring where they fell through now had something blocking the opening.

"Do you think George Hearn shot at us?" Nicole's soft question made him pause. "Did he lure us here?"

Troy glowered at the unknown obstruction. "It crossed my mind." But it made no sense.

"Why would a county employee—"

"He might not *be* a county employee." The statement tumbled out in a rush of clarity. Troy hadn't heard the phone call so he only had Nicole's impression, but his theory made sense after arriving at the abandoned place. It was truly deserted. Not a government vehicle in sight.

A catch of air sounded behind him. "I didn't even think of that," she whispered. "Why does he want to kill us?"

The first few frenzied minutes of their arrival replayed in his mind. Now that he wasn't in the thick of it, his objectivity surged...and what he saw didn't match his first impression. "I don't think we were the target." He allowed the thought to settle.

"How can you say that?" Her protest bounced off the walls. "All those bullets weren't enough?"

Flattening his palms onto the smooth surface above, he guessed it to be at least one of the granite countertops. Maybe all of them stacked on top. He pushed upward. Nothing moved. Not even a small shift. Sucking in a breath, he shoved with all his might. His muscles strained. He tried until he couldn't anymore. No change.

Exhaling, he shook his arms. His mind replayed the first minute again. "The shooter could have nailed either of us with that initial shot, but he took out the tire instead." Then riddled the truck with holes. Why?

"You're right."

Her awed tone snapped his head her approximate way. She didn't have to sound so amazed at his logic. He was a detective after all. Mentally battered, physically dinged, and probably burned out, for sure, but he still had a few working brain cells left.

He turned, inadvertently smacking the front of his boot into something that fell over with a thud.

"Woof."

He crouched, and searched, smacking into hard plastic. "No biggie, Waffles. Just an empty multi-gallon tub." It wobbled, making a weird noise. He rolled it away and scraped the dirt. His fingertips rubbed across cool metal. His Beretta. The impulse to kiss it was strong. He refrained, *barely.* The rush of relief at having a worthy weapon to protect Nicole didn't wipe away his inadequacies, but it lessened the sting. Moving his holster, he resituated his gun on his right side and tucked his shirt out of the way for a faster draw.

A wet nose booped him on the forearm. "How you doing?" He flattened both hands into the dog's fur, instantly finding comfort. A wet lick coated Troy's cheek.

"I'm okay," Nicole answered, not realizing he was talking to the dog.

"You hurt anything?" Smoothing his palms over Waffles's body, the dog flinched when Troy stroked his left front leg.

"I'm sore, but I can walk." Nicole's voice sounded farther away.

Troy frowned. "Waffles is hurt."

"What?" Jogging footsteps grew closer. "Where? How bad?"

"Be careful—"

Nicole yelped as something smacked the wall.

"—there's debris," he finished.

"No kidding," she muttered.

He didn't bother hiding his grin. She couldn't see it anyway. A part of him hoped she'd launch into another random confession. He hadn't understood the reason for the first one, but he learned enough to widen his smile. She thought him pretty with irresistible magnetism and that he smelled good. Mental fist pump.

The air beside the dog intensified. A waft of…summer hit him. He couldn't articulate Nicole's scent other than every time he inhaled it, he thought of warm sunshine and the ocean.

"Waffles." The dog's fur shifted as she combed it.

The Swissador whined.

"Front driver's side leg." A pang shot through Troy's heart at the dog holding his paw off the ground.

"Where?" Her fingers bumped into his. He let go so she could inspect freely.

"Left front," he clarified, still imagining the dog's legs as seats in a car with the head being the windshield. Seemed obvious to him.

"Woof."

Troy took that as Waffles agreeing with him. Unless you were in a country that drove on the wrong side of the road, then his description was backward. *Let it go.*

"Nothing feels broken," she announced into the growing silence.

Summer overtook his senses. He blinked and carefully lifted a hand in front of him. The tips of his fingers grazed her jaw. So close.

Her skin quivered beneath his touch.

When had he leaned forward?

She stilled.

He did the same.

Anticipation and questioning thickened around them.

A small puff of air caressed his lips, her mouth within centimeters of his.

He savored the exchange, spreading his fingertips.

A tremor rippled as her breath caught.

Her body language invited him to close the gap.

Kiss her. No. Yes. Not like this, in the dark like a dirty secret.

Jolting to his feet, he scrubbed his face. "Bad news." He did his best to wrangle his conflicting desires into submission. "The hole is blocked. We can't climb out."

Chapter Twelve

What just happened? Nicole smoothed a finger over her jaw, her breathing erratic.

The hole is blocked. His words smashed through the daze.

No. Her mind hung an Out of Order sign and left the building. Exhaustion weighted her limbs, and she had trouble processing the roller coaster of emotions. Throwing her arms around Waffles, she hugged him tight.

They couldn't climb out?

Powerlessness robbed her hope as the cold, damp air burrowed deeper in her bones.

Waffles wiggled. His large head craned, then he licked her elbow. Forearm. Elbow. Somehow both together.

"Thanks, big guy," she whispered into his back, thawing at his antics. God gave her this beautiful creature to slice through the grief, and He brought Troy just when she needed help—yesterday and today. Smoothing her hands over the dog's soft coat repeatedly, she found the desolation dulling. The three of them were still alive and relatively healthy, and that was enough for now.

Gathering his leash, pain raged through her muscles as she forced them into use. Finally on her feet, she swayed. *Hello, Dizziness, my new frenemy.*

"I don't think we're in a hole," she blurted, pushing the black back with sound. Distraction worked last time.

Clothing rustled and the smell of musk grew stronger. Troy's scent added to the balm Waffles had started. Intense masculinity rubbed against her personal bubble, goosebumping her skin. Troy almost kissed her. The suspense and uncertainty had crackled, heightening the precious moment. But he hadn't and that was for the best. Something deeper inside her reached for him, and she couldn't let it rule her heart. Her brain had to remain in charge until she understood what happened with her uncle. She couldn't accept he was a criminal, but the investigation had her questioning her judgment.

Scratching Waffles's ears, she refocused from veering wildly off-topic in her head. "I did a bit of investigating while you were doing...whatever."

"Seeing if we could climb out."

"Okay. While you were doing that."

"What did you find?"

"I didn't go far, but I think we're in a tunnel."

"Tunnel," he repeated as if contemplating the possibility. "I can't decide if that's good or bad."

"I get it." She pushed a tangle of hair out of her face. "We're either trapped in a hole with no food, water, and unknown quantity of air." Her stomach rolled. "Or we have to travel through a *pitch-black* underground shaft of dubious origin." Her imagination exploded with terrifying movie and book plots coming to life. "We have no clue where it ends, *if* it ends. This thing could be unstable, crushing us to death."

Once she got started, she couldn't stop. "Or we could fall through another hole, breaking our legs or necks or both. Or be stuck in an endless maze. We could become impaled on stalacites or stagamites... How do you say those words?" She swished an agitated hand. "Doesn't matter—"

"Nicole." Troy bopped her left shoulder. Large, warm hands readjusted to squeeze her biceps. "Breathe."

"We should conserve—"

"We'll be fine."

"How do you know?"

"I don't." He exhaled. "But we can't agonize about the

'what-ifs.' We've ruled out escaping back through the cabin floor, so we search for another way. The shooter is still out there, and he might have heard the crashing. I don't want to be here if he investigates."

A whole new round of worries tackled her brain.

"I vote we follow the tunnel." His hold tightened. "Waffles smelled something. I'm trusting the dog didn't lead us to a dead end."

"Literally," she muttered under her breath. "Fine." She thrust her shoulders back. "Let's go."

"Do you have a hold of his leash?"

"Absolutely," she growled, more at the dog than the detective. "I'm not letting go again."

"Woof." Waffles bumped against her leg.

"I hope you have a really good reason for this, buddy." Her grip on the leash tightened. "I hate dark places. Like seriously *haaaate* them."

"Woof."

"I hope you can see," her nerves rambled at the dog, "because you're leading this train. Go on, Waffles." She took a tentative step. "Show me what you smelled."

Julien hustled away from the cabin. Access to the underground tunnel had been sufficiently blocked as if by divine intervention. Julien couldn't have orchestrated a better trap if he tried. Just when he needed it, too.

Nicole Witten was supposed to come alone. He planned on using menacing threats and impressive gun waving to reduce her into a quivering mess. Once he extracted the answer to the riddle and obtained the treasure, she'd experience a tragic death. Something that looked natural and didn't involve an investigation.

Where did the dog come from? Why did she bring it and the cop from yesterday?

His boot slipped on the moss coating rocks within the

terrain. Catching a tree branch in front of him, he managed to stay upright.

The cop wasn't in uniform—it hit Julien. The twit was dating the cop, and the dog belonged to the guy.

Wait. Ice slithered down his spine. Did the twit run to the authorities this morning after they hung up?

Nah. This place would've been crawling with uniforms and suits by now. Most likely the twit told her boyfriend, and he insisted on accompanying her. Not ideal. Not ideal at all.

Julien descended a wonky slope filled with vegetation.

According to paperwork he found inside the single-wide trailer used as an office, the construction company planned to hide the existence of the tunnels beneath the retreat center. At the time, he thought that shady but not his problem. Now, he grinned. With the twit and the cop trapped inside, he had time and options.

Thanks to an old map with that paperwork, he knew exactly how to intercept the trio.

Waffles trotted, his gait skewed with a slight limp.

"Why do you hate the dark?" Troy asked, entwining their fingers together.

She jumped at the intimacy. "Um." Her fingers were stiff. She was shocked at how great it felt but not understanding why he did it.

"Relax," he soothed. "I'm not making a move or anything smarmy. I don't want us to get separated."

"Awful quick to tell me you're not hitting on me, Detective." She kept her tone light so he'd know she wasn't upset. Distraction. Distraction. Distraction kept the heavy darkness from smothering. "Are you afraid of little ole me?"

"Absolutely terrified." Troy laughed, the decadent sound caressing her eardrums.

"Because I called you pretty?" She had to make fun of

her runaway mouth. "Or maybe it was my calling out your showering habit. Admit it, you're a one-bottle man, aren't you?"

"Guilty." The humor in his voice said he felt no need to change.

With the darkness robbing her vision, her other senses heightened. The dank stench grew stronger while a soft, constant noise emanated on the other side of Troy.

"You find me *pretty*—" he bumped her shoulder "—which is not very masculine, by the way, and I find you beautiful."

"Oh. Um. Thank you." A blush heated her face and crept down her neck. Hallelujah, he couldn't see it. Her ego wanted to hear more. "I'm blatantly changing the subject before I get myself in trouble."

"Spoilsport." His light tone battled the darkness pressing on her.

The soft noise morphed into a dull rubbing. "What is that sound? Are you doing something?"

"What, this?" The original noise intensified.

"Yes." She stupidly pointed, jerking Waffles's leash. "What *is* that?"

"Um." He cleared his throat. "I kind of hate not seeing where we're walking."

"Right there with you." Nicole shuddered. "I miss my phone. The flashlight app would be so handy right now."

"Agreed." Troy pumped her hand, sending more goose bumps over her arm. "Call it a control thing, but touching the side keeps me centered. I know it won't help us navigate, but…"

"I get it." And she did, if only she could reach her side of the tunnel. "So, you know all about me—"

"Not even close."

She ignored the statement. "Do you have any brothers or sisters?"

"I'll answer your questions if you answer mine."

"Deal." She liked discovering the different facets of Troy Hollenbeck. Intimidating, smart, shrewd, fun, and playful. Magnetic, haunted—

"I have a twin brother and older sister."

"You have a twin?" Nicole perked up. "Are you identical?"

"Nope." He popped the *p*. "Much to the disappointment of everyone who asks. We're fraternal twins."

"That is so awesome." She'd always wanted a sister or brother, but how cool would it be to have a twin?

"Chase."

"Woof." Waffles pulled on the leash.

"Hey." She yanked the dog back. "No running."

"Sorry." Troy chuckled, helping her settle the dog. "Waffles, that wasn't a command. That's my brother's name."

"You close?" She settled back into a steady walk.

"For thirty-six years. Since we've been womb-mates."

Laughter erupted. "Womb-mates! That's hysterical. So is the twin connection real? Can you tell if he's hurt or happy?"

Chapter Thirteen

Troy understood the curiosity but always floundered for answers. He'd never known a second without Chase. How would he know what was normal or not? "I'm sensing you don't have any siblings."

The tunnel had slowly been descending but now leveled off. Packed-dirt walls competed with long sections of rock. Who built this shaft? Was it engineers or stalwart mountain folk? Which was better? And how long ago?

"None."

He sensed her longing. "Which would you want? A brother or sister?"

"Ohhhh. Hmmmmm." Their connection jiggled. "I don't know. Growing up, I wished for a sister to play with and share secrets, but as I got older, I wanted a brother. He could help me figure out the mystery of boys."

"We are nowhere near as complicated as girls."

"Ha! Says you. Of course a *boy* would argue against the truth."

"I smell a no-win confrontation on the horizon." Troy followed a rough curve in the tunnel. "Subject change. You spent summers in Bell Edge with your aunt and uncle…" How did he word his question without sounding rude or nosy?

A sigh wafted through the space. "It's weird, right?" She barreled on before he could answer. "My dad was an Air Force pilot."

Was. A small hitch panged Troy's heart.

"He died in a training accident when I was two." Sadness crept into her tone. "I don't remember him. Just a few impressions, but nothing real I can hold on to and relive over and over, you know?"

He couldn't imagine. His father was a hard man, but he was an active presence in Troy's life. "I'm sorry." The platitude meant nothing, and he hated that he even offered it.

She shrugged, the motion carrying through their link. "My mom wasn't bad… She couldn't handle raising me on her own. She's always been a successful commercial real estate agent. Her schedule varied so much she had trouble keeping babysitters. When Uncle Ross and Aunt Suzanne offered to watch me over the summers, my mom jumped on it. And I'll be honest, I looked forward to those months of escape, too."

Losing a primary foundation… He just couldn't imagine it. Add to it no siblings to lean on, and she had been a lonely child.

"But it wasn't all morose and angsty," she rallied. "My mom and I found common ground on certain topics like school dances and after-school functions. And my aunt and uncle really made a difference in my life." Her voice wobbled and she sniffed. "My childhood was unconventional, but in the end it worked."

His heart constricted. She had just lost another primary foundation, and before she had a chance to grieve, the FBI descended, crawling all over her inheritance, searching for a way to connect the man to a twenty-five-year-old heist.

"You're impressive, you know that?" He stopped and turned toward her. Guestimating his aim, he found her cheek and swiped a tear away.

"I'm a wreck." She laughed through her tears, then sniffed.

"You're courageous," he countered. "You've been hit with a lot lately and haven't given up."

"I'm a better actress than I thought." Another sniff. "I'm

barely hanging on. I'm afraid of the dark and confessed you have appealing magnetism. Among other things."

He resumed their pace with a huge grin splitting his lips. "I can't say I'm upset to hear what you really think of me."

"Cad." She thumped his hip with their clasped hands. "You should be forced to reciprocate."

"Woofwoofwoof," Waffles alerted, no playfulness in the bark.

Unease stole Troy's mirth. "What, big guy?" Was someone else in the tunnel? Had the shooter found a way to get to them? Or could it be an animal? The image of them stumbling into a bear drained the blood from his head. He swayed, swallowing hard.

The reassuring rocky wall disappeared from his touch. His fingertips tingled, so used to rubbing against a hard surface. "Waffles, stop."

Scratching paw-nails ceased. The dog whined.

"What is it?" Nicole pulled on their link as if twisting.

"I don't know." Dankness seeped into his bones, uncomfortable and clammy.

He held his breath, straining to hear anything out of place. Waffles panted loudly, and Nicole's shoes kicked pebbles or something equally small, sending them skittering. He concentrated on blocking their sounds. Tinkling water caught his attention.

"I think there's a stream or water coursing down a rock wall." He couldn't tell which direction the water flowed, but the peaceful melody took the edge off his anxiety.

"I hear it," Nicole breathed, bouncing their hands.

He stretched his right arm. Emptiness. "Is this space larger?" He dropped Nicole's hand.

"Hey." She knocked into his wrist, searching for him.

"I'm not going far." He paced to the right. The wall should be…he held his palms out…right there. It wasn't.

Waffles whined again, then added a low, rolling growl as if trying to tell them something.

The hair on the back of Troy's neck stood.

"Nicole," he hissed. "Don't move."

A sharp intake of breath, then silence.

Turning slowly, careful to keep his movements muted, he stared. Hard. The blackness refused to abate. He inhaled. A new scent coated his nose…no, not new…amplified. Musty, dank dirt and old wood had an overwhelming layer of minerals from stone.

"Hoooowwwwlll," Waffles called.

Troy jumped at least a foot.

The dog mewled.

What did Waffles scent? Indecision cemented Troy's boots to the ground. Did he leave Nicole or take her with him to investigate? Which risked her safety more?

The oppressive darkness yielded no answers.

A soft touch grazed his heart.

He jolted, fear blasting his veins like ice-fire.

"Sorry," Nicole whispered, balling his T-shirt.

He exhaled, the synapses in his brain still bursting with conflicting instructions: run, fight, duck, jump, have a heart attack. Definitely going to sport gray hair by the end of the day.

A wet nose scraped across his forearm, followed by a low *ruff.*

"Waffles pulled me." Uncertainty colored her tone. "I know you said to freeze, but I didn't want to let go of the leash."

"It's fine." He wrapped a hand around her trembling wrist.

He couldn't leave her behind. Separating now left them both vulnerable. "Stick close to me, okay?" He curbed the urge to stroke her hair.

"No problem." Her whispers puffed against his skin. "Are we in a cavern or something? It seems bigger."

At least he had confirmation Nicole felt the vastness, too. "I can't tell. Could be an intersection."

"Great," she drawled flatly. "My maze theory coming to life."

He pumped her small wrist. "I'd ask what your favorite maze movie is, but I can't think of a single one that doesn't involve terrible tragedies or horrors."

"Your pep talk needs work, Detective." She patted his biceps.

Waffles whined and butted Troy's forearm. *"Woof."*

Troy interpreted that to mean, *stop stalling.* "Hold on to the back of my shirt." Once he felt a weight in the material, he put both hands out and took a step forward.

Chapter Fourteen

A long shiver of foreboding stole from the crown of Nicole's head to her sweaty-yet-freezing toes. The oppressive darkness grew and expanded with every step.

"Troy." She pulled on his shirt. "Stop a second."

He did immediately, twisting. "Everything okay?"

"What's the plan? Are we just going to wander until we run into something?"

He shifted. She let go of the material, and a wall of male heat stood within inches, warming her front. The impulse to wrap him around her like a blanket raged strong.

"Woofwoofwoof." Waffles paced to the end of the length, indicating they should move.

She bumped Troy's stomach. "He's leading deeper toward the left."

Clothing rustled, then the heat wall disappeared just as his big hand entwined with hers again. One of the knots at the top of her spine loosened. She craved the comfort and security of his warm skin against hers. Not that she'd admit it out loud… Okay. Fifty-fifty chance she might as a distraction.

Three steps into the vast unknown, a loud thud lifted her off the ground in an impressive jump.

"Troy?" she croaked around her heart in her throat.

Air sucked through clenched teeth as he squeezed her hand. "That hurt," he groaned.

Before she could ask, Troy swung their clasped hands forward, knocking her knuckles into something hard.

"Ow." She wiggled her hand free and felt along the obstruction. Yelping at a pinch on her fingertip, she shook her hand. Splinter. Okay. Wood, not rock, about waist height. The surface vibrated as she continued exploring. Round with…some kind of metal strap. "A barrel?"

"I think so." Troy's inspection took his heat beyond reach. "I found something."

"Grrrrrrrrrrrrrroooooooowwwwwwl. Wooooof." Waffles tugged.

She lost her balance and smacked her palm on top of the barrel to keep from falling over.

"Careful," Troy warned, just as she heard a chilling sound.

A striking match.

"Troy!"

Too late. A spark ignited.

Nicole dropped, pulling Waffles with all her might. The dog resisted, then ran toward her. She threw her arms around the canine, tucking her head against his coat. *Please, God, save our souls—*

"What are you doing?"

"We didn't die! *Whoop.*"

"Why would we die?" Troy asked.

She opened her eyes. "I can see." Darkness still oppressed the space, but they had a four-to-five-foot radius where dim yellow beat it back. In front of her face perched a weathered wooden cask reeking of vinegar and other scents she couldn't define. Beside it were more barrels, grimy glass, and pottery jugs. *A lot* of jugs.

"Hey." He poked her shoulder. "You thought I'd kill us? Where's the faith, Witten?"

Glaring upward, she cataloged the dirt and grit coating his skin, hair, and clothes. How could he still look so good when he should look ridiculous?

It wasn't fair. She bet she resembled a fork in a light socket victim crossed with a mud-patty connoisseur. Her ire deepened. "Ever heard of fumes trapped in underground tunnels,

Hollenbeck?" She let go of Waffles. "They explode. We have no idea what's fermenting down here."

"I think I've got a good idea."

Troy's curious response drained her grumpy worry.

"You do?" She jumped to her feet—well, more like wobbled with protesting aches. Her focus zeroed in on an antique glass-and-dented-metal lamp resting on top of the battered barrel.

"Turn around." Troy swirled his finger.

Waffles backed up, getting between her legs. She slapped a palm on the edge of the barrel and cringed when it swayed as if about to collapse.

Troy snatched the lamp up by the wonky wire handle.

"Let's try this again." Nicole readjusted the leash, then swung a leg over the back of the dog as she turned.

Tall vague shapes in a confusing configuration stood in the shadows. The light only revealed pieces. "What is that?"

"Waffles's nose is more refined than I suspected."

The hushed awe had her cocking her head, but the gesture didn't add enlightenment.

"He led us to moonshine. Hooch. White lightning. Firewater. Take your pick of names." Troy lifted the lantern. "I grew up about an hour west of here."

Nicole snapped her gaze onto his face. "Really?"

He nodded. "These mountains used to be riddled with homegrown distilleries brewing corn whiskey. Prohibition didn't slow the distillers down. Just made the shiners inventive." The light jiggled with his arm movements. "Makes sense with a stream nearby." His eyes twinkled. "Do you know what this means? We're in the bootleggers' tunnel system."

"Corn whiskey," Nicole repeated, stuck on the beginning of his explanation. "Fermentation." She jolted. "*Ethanol.* That's *fuel.*"

"Yup." His grin widened. "Works great." He raised the lamp. "See."

She couldn't breathe. "Troy, that *blows up.*" Her heart slammed against her ribs. "Like a bomb." Her gaze dropped to Waffles. "Holy moly… I've got a bomb-sniffing dog. Waffles finds stuff that explodes." The implications crashed through the disbelief. "And we followed him."

"Relax." Troy's posture practiced what he preached. "This setup has been here for *decades.*" A hand swished toward the cobweb-infested still.

She shuddered and tried to block the existence of the owners of those webs.

"That hasn't been used in forever." Troy lowered his arm. "There's nothing brewing, ergo, no flammable gas in the air."

"But there're matches." She jabbed a finger toward a box on top of a barrel. "And the flame in that lantern."

"Nicole." Troy faced her. "Give me a little credit."

Embarrassment heated her insides. She had basically accused the man—a trained police officer who handled weapons—of being careless with a lamp. Inhaling to fight the panic, she dipped her chin. "Sorry."

"Woof. Woof. Woof. Woof." Waffles's eyes stared at something beyond the light. *"Grrrrrrrrrrrrrrrrrr."*

Every cell she owned blitzed fire and ice.

Troy positioned himself in front of her.

She grabbed the back of his shirt and stepped to the left.

He glowered over his shoulder, but she ignored the warning. She knew the drill by now and wasn't leaving his side. The lantern illuminated a new section, and she refused to miss it.

The weak lighting didn't reach very high, but from what she could tell they were in a natural rock cavern. She sensed it was spacious, which made her feel a little better. Not only did it lessen the oppressiveness, but it also accommodated more air to dissipate lingering gases.

More of the rickety still came into view, but she didn't care.

What or who had Waffles growling?

Chapter Fifteen

❧

"*Grrrrrrrowl.*" The scruff on Waffles's neck rose.

Adrenaline flooded Troy's veins, amplifying his sight, smell, and hearing, but also messing with his coordination. If he didn't have diligent training, he'd probably drop the lantern and fumble with his hands. As it was, his body betrayed him with a shiver he couldn't hide thanks to the flame flickering with his movements.

He glared into the weak lighting. Wood, metal, and copper shone from the oversize still, but too many shadows remained. His free palm itched to pull his gun, but he didn't. If he needed to fight or help Nicole, he didn't want both hands full. As it was, he longed to ask Nicole to take the light to leave his arms free, but that wouldn't be fair. She already had to control the dog, and he wanted her to hang on to his shirt.

Peering over his shoulder, he cataloged her status. Tangled hair stuck out in places and brimmed with debris. Dirt streaked her face but didn't hide the pasty skin, and her clothing no longer had any semblance of clean. In a word: *beautiful.*

Realigning his priority, he shot her a warning look and mouthed, *Stay behind me.*

She nodded, her movements jerky. Fear had blown her pupils so wide they overpowered her gray irises.

Pebbles skittered ahead, the sound barely reaching Troy's heightened hearing.

"*Woofwoofwoofwoof.*" Waffles pulled Nicole's arm straight, zeroing in on the still. Whatever or whomever approached on the other side of the five-foot-tall home-made contraption.

Waffles chuffed, craning his neck to peer at Troy. The look in his brown eyes said, *What are you waiting for? Let's go.*

Right. The only way to protect Nicole was to know the threat. He motioned to the dog to show him what he sensed.

Waffles licked his chops and took a step forward. Troy did the same.

Stilted breathing hitched behind him, but Nicole remained silent.

Waffles wove a path through the strewn moonshine supplies and empty jugs, determined to find his quarry.

No stalagmites grew from the ground, and Troy wondered if Nicole was happy or disappointed one of her predictions didn't pan out.

Shadows danced at the edge of the light, and he finally glimpsed the rock wall ahead. The cavern was generous, and the ceiling soared beyond the yellow light's reach. How far they had traveled from the construction site, he had no clue, but they were deep inside the mountain.

Lamplight bounced off the end of the roundish still that had a funky lid with copper coiling over to a tall wooden tub, decrepit with age.

Waffles slowed, his head lowering, a menacing growl erupting from his chest.

Nicole tightened her fist on Troy's shirt, straying a little too far beyond his body. He preferred she stay right behind him but realized that was folly. She had to keep an eye on the dog, but he wanted to shield her.

Heart pounding, he braced for…anything. Clearing the side of the copper, he scoured the ground. More barrels, jugs, and other detritus.

"Woof. Woof. Woof. Woof." Spittle flew from Waffles's mouth.

Movement had Troy snapping his gaze forward. A man wearing boots, dirt-patched jeans, and a button-down shirt stood next to a grouping of barrels.

Nicole gasped.

"Woofwoofwoofwoof." Waffles pulled on the leash.

Nicole slammed into Troy's back, her arm stretching forward.

Troy grabbed a section of nylon. "Waffles."

The dog instantly ceased straining but didn't stop glowering at the newcomer.

Neither did Troy. "What are you doing here?"

"I could ask the same of you." The man who broke into Nicole's house yesterday swung a black 9 mm SIG Sauer from behind his back and aimed it at Troy's chest.

Nicole sucked in a breath. Her world narrowed onto the round hole at the end of the gun. Since she was shorter than Troy, the black ring was closer to eye level, sucking all her focus.

Please, God. Her nails scraped Troy's back through the material.

"Grrrrrrrowl." Waffles's scruff rippled as he lowered his head.

"That dog makes one move toward me," the man from her house warned, "it dies."

Terror shot to her bladder. The utter lack of empathy and remorse in those words chilled her blood. *God, please.* She hoped God figured out how to interpret her plea. Her mind barely functioned at the moment.

The intruder appeared close to Troy's age, but the comparison ended there. He stood six feet tall, and his brown hair hadn't seen a comb lately nor had his clothes been inside a washing machine. Dirt covered large parts, but who was she to judge with her filthy shorts and shirt? The man kept his physique trim, but his eyes made her swallow. Practically dead, brown irises beamed their way.

"Let me guess." Troy's posture remained like granite. "There is no George Hearn at the County Planning and Development Division."

The grin that spread the intruder's lips filled her with revulsion. "There is." He cocked his head. "He's on vacation at the moment."

Troy's back muscles rippled. "Permanently?"

The man laughed.

Nicole shivered, resisting the urge to curl against Troy's back to hide from the evil.

"Not this time."

The casual reply about murdering someone dried the last remaining moisture in her mouth.

"Explains how a county employee knew to call you, Nicole," Troy mused softly. "That's been bothering me."

Nicole blinked. Her petrified mind hardly functioned. Hopefully later Troy's statement made sense.

The intruder's free hand disappeared behind him, then came forward with a folded piece of paper. "Recognize this, Nicole?"

She stared at the page with no visible writing. "No." The frail word barely carried, so she tried again. "No."

"Who are you?" Troy demanded.

The man's expression hardened. "I'm not talking to *you*, Cop." The paper jiggled as he adjusted his grip to point at Nicole. "I'm asking *her* questions."

"And she's not answering until you tell me who you are." Troy let go of Waffles's leash.

"Go for that gun and you're dead."

Nicole flinched.

Troy froze.

Waffles growled, low and menacing.

"Be a good boy—" the intruder's tone flipped back to conversational "—and toss your weapon. Now."

Troy didn't move.

Nicole held her breath.

With slow movements, Troy pulled his gun from the holster and tossed it to the right, opposite of the still. It thudded against the rock flooring five feet away.

"As I was saying…" The man fiddled with the paper with one hand until it opened but didn't hang flat. "Recognize it now?"

Cement seemed to replace her cross-trainers, securing her feet to the ground. Forcing her trembling body to slide farther beyond Troy's back, she leaned forward.

"Nicole," Troy hissed, his jaw hard.

She tried to swallow but the dryness burned instead. "I'm—" Her voice cracked. She cleared her throat. "I'm not moving." Staring at the paper, the black ink looked like a bunch of gibberish. The chaos ruling her mind—

"Oh." She squinted. All at once, she grasped what he had in his hands. Violation and grief hit so hard she swayed against the detective. "Where did you get that?"

"Nicole?" Troy twisted. His eyes widened as he threw his right arm around her shoulders. "What is it?" Troy glared at the intruder. "What do you want?"

"Ask your girlfriend." He motioned to Nicole with the gun.

Nicole pushed against Troy's chest until he let go. "You stole it."

"Sure did." The intruder smiled, not caring a bit he held the last remaining connection she had with her uncle. Maybe the only good connection she had left. "Kind of you to leave it on the dresser for me."

Days after she moved in, she couldn't take seeing the file with her uncle's will and other documents every day, so she had placed it in the master bedroom and shut the door.

"Nicole." Troy swiped her cheek, smearing tears she didn't know fell. "What's on the paper?"

Her breath hitched. "The last riddle Uncle Ross invented for me."

Chapter Sixteen

"Riddle?" Troy's gaze slid from the page to the guy's oily smile. The expression showed how much he enjoyed inflicting pain and loved watching Nicole on the verge of falling apart.

"For as long as I can remember—" Nicole sniffed "—my uncle created riddles for me to solve." Her breathing stuttered. "Every summer he'd present me with a new one. It was our thing." Tears coursed down her cheeks.

Troy wanted to rip the paper from the intruder's hand and punch the vicious smile off his face.

"Awwww." The man puckered his lips. "So sweet. Gag." He faux retched, then lowered his arm. "Want to trade memories? I knew your beloved uncle Ross in Chicago."

Troy stiffened as Nicole clutched his forearm.

Waffles growled.

"The Syndicate lost one of the best fences in the business when Ross retired to this backwoods area. He was a genius at selling and transporting stolen items."

"What?" Nicole gasped, squeezing Troy's arm. "You're lying."

In a flash, the intruder's eyes deadened. "Accuse me of that again and you'll regret it."

Fear slid down Troy's spine. The guy was a psychopath; he had demonstrated no sense of morality or empathy and made clear he had a huge ego in the short span of their conversation. This situation had gone from bad to nightmare in a blink.

"Ask your boyfriend." The psycho motioned to Troy with his gun. "The FBI investigated Witten before for money laundering on top of a long list of other offences, but Ross was too slick."

"No." Nicole shook her head. "My uncle was a great man—"

"Yes, he was," Psycho interrupted. "At making The Syndicate money and keeping Salvatore Ricca out of jail. Even my father revered the guy." His lips twisted into a scowl. "Thank God they both died before they learned of Ross's betrayal."

A thousand scenarios to disarm Psycho flittered through Troy's mind, but he discarded them as fast as they arrived. Troy's priority was Nicole. He couldn't jeopardize her safety.

"What betrayal?" Nicole's grip bit into his arm.

"Are you really this dumb?" Psycho shifted a sneer at Troy. "You're either seriously hard up or you and this twit don't spend time talking."

"Knock it off." The lamp's wire handle bit into Troy's palm.

"I'll spell it out for you, pretty twit." The madman talked slowly. "Ross stole the Viking artifacts."

"No, he didn't," Nicole shot back.

"Who's your father?" Troy asked before she closed her mouth.

"Nice try." Psycho grinned, his mood flipping like a switch. "You don't need to know a thing about me…well, maybe one thing." His tone was lackadaisical.

Troy's skin crawled. He'd dealt with a lot of criminals and lowlifes in Philly, but he'd never met a true psychopath.

"Cross me, you die. Prevent her from solving this—" he lifted the paper "—you die horribly. Don't keep control of the dog, it dies, then you. Understand?"

The intruder's dead eyes reflected he meant every word.

Psycho flexed his fingers around the grip of the SIG Sauer. Not once had his muscles shown signs of fatigue or stress from holding it in place. That meant too much practice and experience.

"Now." The intruder shook the page. "Let's get started. Read this out loud so your boyfriend can play along with the rest of the class."

Nicole leaned forward. "I can't see it."

Psycho rolled his eyes. "Take it, you twit."

A harsh tremor rocked Nicole's body.

"I'll—"

"Did you already forget the rules?" Psycho cut Troy off. "Don't interfere." His gaze slid to Nicole. "I don't have all day."

"Grrrrrrrowl. Woof. Woof. Woof."

"Control the dog or I will."

Troy took the leash from Nicole, hating that both his hands were full—no—loathing the terrified woman had to step closer to insanity.

Waffles tried to move when Nicole took a step, but Troy muscled him in place.

Nicole snatched the paper from Psycho's fingers, then hustled backward.

The moment she bumped into Troy's arm, he exhaled. "Read it."

The paper shook as she spread it open.

Troy tuned out Nicole's whispered words. It inflamed him too much to listen to her fear. Instead, he read the masculine scrawl over her shoulder.

I know, I know. You hate hints. I can hear you howling, Nicole, but indulge an old man. Start the hunt here: a set of latitude and longitude numbers were listed.

I babble and chatter.
I dabble and lather.

I have various moods.
I cut and intrude.
Do you know what I am?

The heavens and trees
are nowhere in me.
Whether high or low,
I've wended and stowed.
Do you know what I am?

My names are many and wide.
I've been celebrated and denied.
My light pales despite the sun's rays,
yet Witten offers me praise.
Do you know what I am?

When all put together
these clues lead to treasure.

She dropped her arms, the riddle dangling from her hand. Grief stole her stance and expression, leaving Troy helpless. He couldn't hug her or offer comfort, and it sliced surprisingly deep.

"Treasure," Psycho hummed. "Exactly." The SIG Sauer shifted to Nicole's chest. "You robbed me of what's rightfully mine, so it's only fair I return the favor."

The sword. If Troy had to guess, he'd bet this guy's father was the one who killed the two security guards the night of the heist.

"It's a lot of pretty language to slog through, but you're going to tell me where the treasure is."

Nicole didn't move or react. Her chest expanded and contracted so fast, she was going to hyperventilate.

"She needs fresh air." Troy itched to set the lamp down. "How did you get here? We fell through the flooring."

Psycho narrowed his eyes on Nicole. "Is she going to throw up?"

Troy ignored the flat question. "Can we exit the way you came?"

"Sure. I have an old bootleggers' map." He patted a back pocket.

Troy lifted the lamp. Yellow light flung toward the walls, causing shadows to become blacker. If he squinted, he could make out two other large openings. One behind the intruder and one to the right. Casks, crates, jugs, and debris littered the area, but nothing seemed to block the actual exits.

It was now or never.

He dropped Waffles's leash. Blowing out the flame, he set the lamp down, then snatched Nicole.

"Waffles, attack," he commanded as he clutched her to his chest and ran.

Waffles snarled.

Gunfire rent the black cavern.

A barely human scream bounced off the walls.

Chapter Seventeen

Nicole snapped out of the haze and jammed the riddle into her side pocket. She threw her arms around Troy's neck to keep her balance as her brain sloshed with every jostling step.

Gunfire echoed. *Crack. Crack. Crack.*

Terror blitzed her body. Overwhelming darkness hid the trajectory of the shots.

Waffles snarled, the merciless sound goose-bumping her skin.

An agonized scream followed.

"Waffles," Nicole bellowed, desperately searching the dark.

Troy smacked into something hard. Scraping resounded as strong arms ripped away. She dropped, her ribs smacking against a solid edge, rolling her.

Yelping, she tried to stop herself with her hands. Her palms bounced off wood, then smashed into jugs that shifted and toppled. Landing in a heap, she grunted.

"Nicole." Troy's pained call came from somewhere to her left.

She sat up, groaning and holding her ribs.

"We gotta move," Troy croaked. Jugs thudded against the rock floor.

"Nicole," the intruder shouted.

Adrenaline lanced her veins.

"Woof. Woof. Woof."

Crack. Another gunshot.

"Waffles." Nicole ignored the fresh pain. Using a crate, she hoisted herself upward.

A wet nose bopped her forearm, then a lick followed.

Thank You, God. Tears leaked down Nicole's cheeks as she inspected every inch of her new best friend. No bullet wounds.

Finding the leash, she whispered, "Show me Troy." She prayed the dog understood what she needed. They hadn't been together long enough for her to know which commands the dog had learned, but desperation ruled.

Waffles led her to the left. Her cross-trainers found two more jugs, sending them skittering as her toes cried in misery.

"Hey, big guy," Troy groaned in a soft voice. "Where's your mom?"

"Right here." She bent with her arm outstretched. "Take my hand."

Fumbling seconds later, warm skin gripped hers. She tugged. Her overtaxed muscles from too much yard work quivered, but she kept pulling.

"Nicole," the insane man yelled. "That treasure is *mine*." Grating objects scraped behind her. "You can't escape. You hear me? You're trapped."

Troy swayed but stayed upright.

"I'll find you," the guy continued. "Everything you own belongs to *me*."

Nicole ignored the ranting. She laced her fingers with Troy's and asked as quietly as possible, "Do you know the way out?"

Troy didn't answer verbally. He squeezed her hand, then shifted to take the lead. Neither of them spoke as they trekked. She tried to pay attention to the tension on the leash. If Waffles swerved, she did her best to match.

Losing the lamplight made the darkness even blacker. Heightened hearing and smell didn't combat the oppression. Now even more was at stake than finding a way out. They had to escape a psychopath.

Through their connection, Troy couldn't hide the limp dominating his steps. She longed to ask about the injury, but terror kept her lips locked together. Her own ribs protested, and her sore toes threatened mutiny.

The space around her condensed. Suffocated. They had left the expansive cavern. *Oh, God. Breathe.*

Troy increased the pace.

Nicole risked running beside him, figuring the tunnel was like the one they traversed before. No supplies or obstacles had slowed their progress then. She prayed that held true now.

Ripe earth, minerals, and stale air invaded her nose and coated the back of her throat. Her back muscles twitched, expecting a bullet any second. Could they outrun a madman?

They had to try.

Waffles veered to the left.

Nicole followed suit, pulling on her link with Troy. He didn't react fast enough. His boot slammed into something hard. It scraped against the rock floor until it silenced after a thud.

Fear shot to her abused bladder. No way could the madman miss that sound.

Troy regained his footing, muttering something too low for her to hear.

Every nerve tingled. Even her hair prickled.

Danger. Her instincts screamed at her to run. Her feet couldn't go any faster in the thick darkness.

The leash suddenly slackened.

"Troy." Nicole yanked on their grip, slowing.

"We can't stop," he whispered. His breathing barely registered the exercise while her lungs screamed for more air.

Something hard hit the ground and rolled in front of them.

Oh, Lord. What now?

Waffles whined just as a second, then third…something hit the tunnel floor.

Troy marched forward. She did her best to keep up with his long strides.

Small particles that steadily grew bigger and harder to navigate bit into her soles.

The top of her left shoe slammed into a large, hard object that wobbled, then dropped on top of her foot. *Ye-ow.* Snatching her foot back, she hopped, then threw her arms out to keep her balance.

Troy yanked her toward him, causing the gravelly substances to shift, sliding her leg out from under her. Smacking her nose against a hard chest, she threw her free arm around the detective to keep from hitting the ground.

He staggered backward just as the leash wrapped around her wrist tightened. Waffles bounced, and Troy tripped, dragging her down with him. Only they didn't fall far. Troy's back thumped to a stop at a forty-degree angle with her on top of him. A rain of debris beat against them, the sizes varying from small to large.

"Ow," he groaned under his breath. "My back. My head."

In her scramble to free the detective, she punched his ribs, then shoulder. Large hands gripped her arms and heaved her up as he sat forward.

Finally detangling herself and standing, she followed the length of the leash and unwound it from behind Troy's legs.

Waffles licked her cheek, then whined.

Scratching and scuffing emanated ahead, and Nicole held her breath. *Please don't say we're trapped.*

Troy grunted as rocks hit the floor. "The tunnel's blocked."

Nicole stood and dropped her chin.

Waffles rested his weight against her thigh as if to offer comfort.

Her tingling nerves intensified. They couldn't turn around. They *had* to break through. Pulling her wrist free, she shoved Waffles's leash into Troy's side.

"What—" Troy cut himself off.

She bent at the waist until her palms struck cold hardness. Her skin rippled at the sliminess coating her skin, but she refused to snatch her hands away despite her revulsion. Walking her hands up, she "saw" by touching. Rocks in all shapes and sizes were piled on top of each other with mud and sticks filling in.

"Ni-cole," the intruder sang.

Her palm slipped. Her chin scraped a rock edge.

"Grooooooooowl," Waffles menaced.

"I told you, you can't escape." The voice sounded closer.

She scrabbled upward, jamming her shoes and fingertips into any openings she could find. The back of her head punched the top of the tunnel, ringing her bell. Blinking to clear the pain and disorientation, she started pushing the rocks jammed against the top.

Comeoncomeon, she grunted, using all her strength. Her arms trembled as sweat coated her skin. *Move*, she silently demanded.

"Come now, Nicole," the madman implored, his tone swinging from angry to cajoling. "If you work with me, I promise to make your death painless."

"There's an incentive," she muttered, straining to make headway.

A wall of heat blanketed her right side, and her body instantly recognized Troy. Without a word, he placed a palm near hers and pushed. With their combined effort, the rocks at the top began to wobble.

In the back of her mind, she knew the ceiling could collapse on their heads. The blockage might be the only thing holding it up, but she'd rather risk a cave-in than give in to the psycho.

The rocks shifted, then broke free, tumbling down the other side.

"No, no, no," the madman growled as boots slapped against the ground.

Chapter Eighteen

Troy jabbed at as many rocks as he could reach. His heart remained in his throat, choking his airway. Either the ceiling was coming down, or the psycho would catch up.

Nicole kept working, her pace frenzied.

Stale air slapped his face. Throwing his arm forward, he inspected the opening and realized they had enough space to squeeze through.

Troy touched Nicole's forearm as he leaned next to her ear. "You can slide through."

"Waffles," she breathed.

"I'm going to get him now." Impulse overtook common sense. He lightly kissed the skin at the top of her jaw. His lips barely caressed warm softness.

Her breathing hitched.

"Go." He pumped her forearm. "We'll be right behind you."

"Nicole," Psycho growled. "I will shoot your boyfriend and dog—"

Troy purposefully tuned out the threats. If he didn't, he'd lose the tenuous hold he had on his temper. Nicole and Waffles's safety came first. Once they were somewhere safe, Troy would hunt the madman down.

Finally reaching the bottom, Troy found Waffles with his front paws on the pile. Gathering the leash, Troy helped the dog climb upward. Waffles's tail bashed Troy in the face more times than he could count, but as long as they continued moving, he didn't care.

A vise clamped around Troy's heel. "Gotcha."

Troy pushed Waffles, praying it was enough to reach the

opening. The dog disappeared just as the clamp yanked on his boot. He slid. Crooking his fingers into claws, he managed to stop his descent.

Kicking out with his free leg, he connected with the psycho's head.

The man grunted, losing his grip on Troy.

Snatching his freed leg up, he climbed higher.

"Troy," Nicole hissed, panic filling the word.

Slamming his boots into crevasses, he scrambled to reach the hole.

"Woof. Ruffruffruff." Waffles barked nonstop.

Warm fingers overhead found his. He wanted to howl. She should've run once she had Waffles. *She* was important, not him.

The utter blackness hid too much. He couldn't tell if he knocked the psycho out or if the man was pursuing him.

Either way, Troy could not fail. He had to get Nicole out of the tunnel.

She pulled on his wrist, helping him find the opening. As he shoved his head through, rocks abraded his T-shirt, doing their best to lock him in place. He was larger than Nicole in more than height. His boots slipped on the moss and his knees chaffed on the stone, but he kept wiggling. Two rocks gouging his stomach finally broke free. They acted like a sled, rolling and taking him with them.

The top of his head smacked into Nicole's chest. She yelped as she lost her balance. Together, they slid partway down the pile, until the two stones lost their leverage.

"We have to move," he ground out between clenched teeth, his entire body one large ache.

For a moment he debated filling the hole in, then discarded the idea. They'd only waste precious time. Once loose, Psycho would have no trouble breaking through the rocks.

Waffles stopped barking, his nose finding Troy's shin.

Troy rubbed his hand over the dog until he found the leash. His other hand reached outward, connecting to Nicole's hip. "Can you run?"

"Yes." She laced her fingers with his.

"Let's go." It was harder to stand than he wanted to admit, but he kept silent. He didn't matter. She had to focus on escape, not him.

He didn't bother with stealth. The psycho already had an advantage. If the old bootleggers' map really existed, the man knew where the tunnel exited.

Troy matched his stride to hers, which eased the stabbing pain in his shin. His legs were naturally longer, and he kept to a strict workout regime for work. Thanks to slamming into obstacles, he needed the extended stamina to maintain the pace.

He envied people who didn't have to exercise and still looked great. He had to stick to a schedule or his mother's genes kicked in, puffing him up.

Allowing Waffles the full length of the leash, Troy pressed his fingertips against the sidewall like he'd done in the other tunnel. It helped center him in the darkness and gave him a warning if the tunnel turned.

Rotting timbers broke away from nails securing them into the rock walls, stretching into the tight space. Troy avoided smacking a section just as the tunnel curved to the right.

Nicole's breaths became strained and heavier, but he didn't slow.

Natural light ahead beat back the black. *Exit!* his mind cried.

"Woof. Woof." Waffles audibly sniffed.

The curve ended, and a patch of sunlight highlighted stones filling the exit of a cave. Giant boulders piled together, forming a natural barrier to hide the tunnel. A large triangle existed in a configuration they didn't have to climb to get out.

They exploded through one by one with Waffles first, Nicole second, and Troy last.

Decadent scents of pinesap, blooming foliage, decaying limbs, and damp moss invaded his nose. Leafy trees and shrubs swayed in the constant warm breeze. Sunlight pierced through the canopy, causing shadows to move and twist, and dissolved the tunnel's oppressive grip.

He wanted to kiss everything in sight.

No time. They had to disappear.

Julien cradled his injured arm against his chest, cursing the cop. His head throbbed from the kick, and the bite marks on his arm still bled. Stupid dog. First chance he got, he was taking that mutt out of the equation.

Sudden silence ahead slowed his steps. The cop had knocked Julien out, but it must not have been for long. Once he climbed through the opening in the blockage, he could hear their running echoing against the rock walls.

Amateurs. You needed stealth to hide, not speed. This blasted darkness hid everything. If they had pressed against the walls, Julien could've passed them and not known it.

Their stupidity was his gain.

But now… Now he had to be careful. They either found the exit or set a trap.

He smacked into a wall. Choice words flew to his tongue as he bent over. Agony ripped through his arm and head. Letting go of his injury, he rubbed his fingers against the wall, following it around a sharp curve. He probably left blood behind, but who cared? No one would see it.

Finally, light shone ahead. Reaching the exit, he cautiously peered out.

Nothing.

The cop had thrown his gun, so Julien felt confident to stride into the fresh air. He didn't bother searching for the pair. He already knew where they were headed. All he had to do was pick up some supplies from his RV, then settle into his nest. He'd have a front-row seat when they discovered his surprise.

Chapter Nineteen

Nicole gulped air like the forest would run out. Clamping a hand over the stitch in her side, she paced the small area. One, two, three, four, five, boulder. Pivot. One, two, three, four, five, ash tree. Quarter pivot. Four, five, six, seven, overgrown mountain maple.

Chest heave. Heave. Heave. Her lungs gobbled the oxygen, demanding more.

She hated running. With a passion. Not that the pace could be called running. More like jogging, but it counted. All the sweating, bouncing, lack of proper air in her lungs… There was a reason runners never smiled in photos.

Quarter pivot.

Scanning the area, she didn't see or hear Troy. Good. Lifting the bottom of her T-shirt, she wiped her drenched face. Ick. Blood mixing with dirt on the material made her pause. She rubbed her fingers over her throbbing chin. Wetness smeared on her skin. It wasn't much, but still. Open wound in a dirty forest? That just asked for trouble, and she had enough already.

Twigs cracked to her right.

She dropped her T-shirt just as Troy rounded a thick ash trunk.

"I don't see or hear anything."

Her gaze swept over the detective. Dirt coated almost every inch, and a myriad of bruises were going to sport spectacular colors soon. While she sucked in air and couldn't stop trembling in the aftermath of violence, the handsome man appeared calm and collected.

"How do you do it?" she blurted out, rubbing her arms.

He cocked his head, probably noting her every nuance and flaw. He'd find many. "Do what?"

"Your job. This. Whatever." She hugged herself. "I couldn't handle it." Her mouth twisted. "I'm not big into adrenaline rushes, and blood and gore are my downfall. Not exactly helpful for someone wanting to be in the medical field, hence my exciting career as a dental hygienist."

He inched closer. "There's no shame in that." The corner of his mouth quirked. "I couldn't handle being a hygienist."

She snorted. "You don't need to placate me."

"I'm serious." His blue eyes locked on hers. "Listening to those drills all day. Inspecting people's mouths. Handling saliva and bad breath." He shuddered. "No thanks."

"Beats getting shot at."

"I'll give you that." He held out his hand.

She dropped her arms, confused. They weren't in the dark anymore, so why did he want to hold her hand?

"Take it. Please." He stepped closer. "I need the connection."

So did she. More than she wanted to admit. Lacing their fingers, his strength and power seeped into her skin, soothing the maelstrom inside. It took all of her not to close her eyes and bask.

Troy began walking. The forest floor had no discernible trail. Ivy, ferns, and other ground-covering vegetation melded with thick bushes and scrubs, hiding pitfalls ready to twist ankles or tumble them downward.

Waffles wandered ahead, sections of his leash battering the leaves on the profusion of plants.

"Thank you," he said softly, his limp hardly noticeable. "Can I confess something?"

"Sure." This enigmatic man could tell her anything he wanted. He just saved her life.

"I don't know if I should be a police officer anymore."

"Really?" Those were the last words she expected. "You seem really good at it."

The chuckle he emitted relayed hurt and bitterness. "You should run as far away from me as possible." He kicked a dead limb into a patch of ferns. "I used to work in Philadelphia. My last assignment…" His breathing stuttered.

Waves of pain rolled off him, rubbing against her grief.

"Let's just say I failed spectacularly." Another branch soared. "My partner was shot multiple times."

Her hand flew to her mouth, Waffles's leash banging her lips. "Oh, no. He didn't die, did he? Please tell me he's okay."

"Define *okay*." Troy gazed ahead. "He's alive, but he had to retire. He loved his job. Always talked about someone having to physically pry him out of the precinct when he got too old. Thanks to me, that day came at thirty-nine."

Nicole had no clue what to say. She didn't know the details, but she couldn't imagine Troy being at fault.

"The suspect not only shot my partner, he killed a mother and child because they witnessed him execute someone else. I failed them, too."

Her heart bled for him. No wonder his eyes were haunted. He carried the weight of so much guilt. "Troy." She squeezed his hand. "I'm not privy to the circumstances, but I don't believe God set you up to fail."

"You sure?" he snapped. "Because God abandoned those people when He put their lives in my hands."

"You saved *me*."

"Dumb luck." He tried to pull his hand back, but she tightened her grip.

"Divine intervention." She had to get through to him. "Without you, I would be at the mercy of that madman." Chills stole down her spine. "You saved me yesterday, too."

"Again, luck."

"No," she countered. "God gave me you."

"I've seen too much evil to have that kind of faith."

"Then I'll believe for the both of us." She peered up at him. His hard jaw ticked. "God sent you to me." Embarrassment flushed her skin. "I mean, He sent you to help me."

A small crack in his armor appeared. He snorted as a wry smile quirked his mouth. "I like the first statement better."

Warmth for a whole different reason thawed her blood. Distraction time. "Do you know where we're going?" She had lost her sense of direction down in the cavern and tunnels.

"I'm hoping we're headed toward the construction site. I doubt there's a phone, but we should search. If we strike out, that means hiking to find help. I've got an emergency kit with a few bottles of water and some energy bars stashed behind the seats in my truck."

The memory of the barrage of bullets replayed. "Unless they're filled with holes."

He grimaced. "I was trying to be positive."

"Sorry to be a Debbie Downer." Her shoulders slumped.

"Hey." His voice softened. "Are you okay?" He snorted. "Dumb question. Of course you're not. Talk to me." He pumped their connection. "Forget I'm a detective. Right now I'm your friend. Rail if you need it. Cry, although I warn you I'll probably freak out." He inhaled as if to steel himself. "No, I can handle it. Roll the tears. Get it out. You've been hit with too much."

Friend. She needed a friend but…in the short amount of time she'd known him, her soul recognized him as so much more. *Wanted* him to be so much more.

No. Right now he couldn't be anything else. She couldn't handle anything else.

Chapter Twenty

"**I** wish I never dug up that sword," popped out before Nicole realized the thought. Anger pushed out the last of the cold. "If I had just left those stupid bushes alone…" She plucked a pink-and-white flower off a mountain laurel shrub and shredded the petals.

"Woof." Waffles trotted back.

The ground steadily sloped upward, taxing her calves. "Uncle Ross isn't evil."

"Of course not." Troy scowled. "Don't compare him to that psychopath."

"Did you know him?" The anger diffused into longing for someone else to understand, for someone else to know her uncle the way she did.

Her shoe found a depression, throwing her gait off.

Troy pulled her out. "No. Sorry. I moved here two months ago."

"Oh. Right." Disappointment punched her heart. "You just sounded so sure. I thought maybe…"

Troy paused, forcing her to stop as well. Turning to face her, he brushed his thumb over her cheek. "I'm sorry I didn't get to meet him before he passed."

Was he? It was a horrible thought. Yet, law enforcement seemed to enjoy slapping her with accusations and information that conflicted with the man she knew.

Not fair to blame that on Troy. He hadn't said a word… although, he did have that one noticeable pause in the police station.

Gorgeous blue eyes tracked over her face. "That guy in the tunnel is a true psychopath." Another stroke with his thumb. "I mean it. He's the very definition—egotistical, disinhibited, and has no remorse and empathy for others. There is no way your uncle was like that. Not by the way you talk about him or the way you grieve."

"Great." She pulled her cheek away. "So Uncle Ross was not psychotic, just a criminal."

Troy dropped his arm. "I didn't say that."

"Right. You only admitted he wasn't crazy." She ripped her hand from his and began trudging through the vegetation. Leaves tickled her legs, and she prayed none were poisonous. All she needed was a painful rash on top of everything else.

"That's not fair, Nicole."

Waffles strode beside her.

She stopped and dropped her head. "True." Her nose itched as tears threatened to fall. "I'm taking shots at you, and you don't deserve it."

The ground vibrated with his steps. Warm fingers rubbed the top of her spine. "I'm strong enough to take it...*if* it helps."

"It doesn't." She sighed. "I don't want to believe Uncle Ross had anything to do with The Syndicate." She searched his concerned face. "Maybe I'm naive, but it's hard to accept Salvatore Ricca was his only client." A squabbling pair of birds attracted her attention. "Our summers were about the present or things happening in my life. He rarely talked about his work in Chicago. Every now and then he'd mention parties or shows he and Aunt Suzanne attended." She shrugged. "I didn't think anything of it. I mean, he was an attorney. I expected him to keep information secret."

Waffles butted his head against her thigh.

Nicole spread her fingers and combed the dog's fur. "Thanks, big guy." She crouched and hugged the Swissador. "I'm worried."

Troy crouched on the dog's other side. "About what?"

She bit her lip. He might say he was her friend, but he was very much a detective. Did it matter? The FBI probably noted the state of the backyard by now. "When I dug up the sword, I noticed other recently disturbed areas."

His eyes sharpened.

Her stomach knotted. She wasn't accusing her uncle of anything, but it still felt like she was betraying him. "There are four other places in the yard."

"Five total." His mind visibly churned. "That matches the number of stolen items."

She winced. "The FBI is trying to connect my uncle to the heist, and my finding the sword just gave them ammunition to tear his estate apart."

Waffles licked her forehead.

Her nose scrunched at the dirt now coating the poor dog's tongue. She pushed herself upward.

Out of nowhere, the statement Troy made in the cavern popped into her mind. It suddenly made sense. "How did someone in the county office know to call me after Uncle Ross died?" she murmured.

Troy stood, entwining their hands together. "It bothered me when you first told me about the call." He tugged to resume their pace. "If you weren't aware of the retreat center and nothing was provided in the will, how did the county know you were next of kin?"

"It's foolish, but I can't help clinging to the hope that Uncle Ross died before he had the chance to update the will. I inherited everything."

Troy nodded, but the creases around his mouth deepened.

"Spit it out." She rolled her wrist. "What aren't you saying?"

"Your uncle was an attorney." A stiff wind shook the leaves. "He could maintain his own will. I'm betting he had an agreement with the local lawyer on how to retrieve the document in case of emergency. And let's face it, the retreat center's planning and construction began months ago. Well before your uncle died."

Punch to the gut. Nicole absently watched a pair of squirrels chasing each other around a maple trunk.

"Putting the will aside…" Troy took the lead between two close-growing trees. "We have the answer to one mystery."

It took her a moment to think of it. "No one in the county called me. That psycho drew me here."

"Yep."

"And he's the one who told me Uncle Ross invested two-point-six million dollars. How can I trust that? The man's a liar. That could've been another deception to ensure I'd come here. Uncle Ross may have nothing to do with this place."

Troy cleared his throat.

"What?" Nicole's tenuous hope flattened.

"In the riddle your uncle told you to start your search here." He rubbed next to a purpling bruise on his cheek. "He's connected somehow."

The more she learned, the less she knew about Uncle Ross. All her life she believed he was exactly whom he portrayed: an honest man overflowing with love and wisdom.

Eyeing Troy, insidious thoughts slithered from the recesses of her mind. Another "honest" man held her hand. Who really lurked beneath the veneer?

An invisible wall fell over Nicole's features at the same time she untangled their hands.

Instantly missing the warmth and comfort, Troy inhaled against the vise squeezing his chest.

Discussing her uncle this soon after his death would be hard in normal circumstances. Dissecting the man's life and uncovering deception…tragic.

The last thing he should've done was told her about Philadelphia. The confrontation in the cavern, gunfire in the dark, and the fight at the blockade had left him raw. Every decision and movement he had made held her life in the balance. In a moment of weakness, he sought Nicole's vitality and his guard dropped. The confession just sort of poured out.

Now she knew his shame, knew his failures. She'd realize—if she hadn't already—he couldn't protect her. She saw firsthand how his efforts turned out: Richard fought for his life in the hospital, the psycho escaped her house only to lure her to an abandoned site, and she had no way to call for help.

Yeah, Troy was about as useful as one of those clown cops at the circus.

"Nicole." He hustled to block her from walking away. "I'm sorry."

Confusion leaked into her gray irises. "For what?"

Debris stuck out of her tangled hair, and dirt coated her clothing and skin. She should look ridiculous, but she didn't. The dishevelment showed her courage and strength. His respect grew. It took everything he had not to brush his lips over hers. Not to wrap his arms around her and never let go. This woman hooked him thoroughly, and it scared him.

"Troy?" The husky whisper of his name matched the darkening of her irises. "Why are you sorry?"

The list was too long. "You have enough going on." He shunted the list aside. "I shouldn't have unloaded about Phil—"

"Stop." Thunderclouds stormed her features. "Friendships aren't one-sided."

His soul howled. It didn't want to be cast in the friend zone. His mind overrode the dissent. "True—"

"Woof. Ruffffff. Ruffffff. Ruffffff." Waffles tugged the leash, jerking Nicole.

Her shoulder smacked into him, rocking him backward.

Righting himself, he hustled after the two, noticing the sunlight seemed brighter ahead.

In moments, they reached an access road made of gravel and dirt.

Halting on the narrow space between the forest and road, he rested his hands on his hips, adjusting for the empty holster. "Where did this come from?"

"I'm guessing we chose the wrong direction."

The dark tunnels messed with his sense of direction more than he realized. He had no clue how far off they were from the heart of the retreat center.

"I lost track of our distance from the tunnel exit." Nicole shortened the leash to keep Waffles beside her. "Could this be part of the bootleggers' trafficking?" An inelegant noise emanated before a wide smile. "Behold, Hooch Highway."

He laughed, the heaviness inside melting away. New discovery: her wit matched his. "Or Liquor Lane."

Her laugh deepened. "Whiskey Way."

"Rotgut Road." Swiveling to take in the area, he froze.

Silence descended as she shifted to follow his line of sight. "Oh. Um, that's not a mirage, right?"

"No." Suspicion took root.

About a half mile away, an RV was parked in a clearing. The smaller-sized recreational vehicle was perfect for a couple...or one psychotic man.

Troy grabbed Nicole's wrist. "Back into the forest."

He needed to inspect the vehicle, but he couldn't tell if it was empty or not. Better to sneak up on it than become a target by walking down the middle of the road.

Chapter Twenty-One

Julien picked up a pair of binoculars resting next to the sniper rifle. From his vantage high above on a boulder, he had the perfect line of sight to the main retreat center building and the cop's truck.

Julien chuckled at his handiwork. The only way that vehicle was leaving was on a flatbed. He could just picture the tow truck operator's face when he took in all the bullet holes.

Classic. Roving the binoculars, nothing moved outside of the leaves on the surrounding trees. He could wait. Nicole and the detective already proved their combined intelligence didn't come close to his.

Fury swirling just below the surface bubbled to the top. How dare he have to lower himself to her level. That he needed her to solve the riddle added a fresh layer of insult. She'd pay for that offense.

Starting with her boyfriend. The cop butted in where he didn't belong, interfering with Julien's plans. He'd warned the smug guy, yet the detective played hero. Well, tried to, anyway. Blowing out the flame only prolonged the inevitable. Only Julien walked off this mountain alive.

Grazing the knot on his temple, he wished he could return the favor firsthand. He wouldn't mind planting his fist into that *GQ* face, but that didn't fit with his priorities. Isolating Nicole by dispensing with the dog and the cop took precedence.

Refocusing his binoculars on the truck, he had planted a fun surprise—

Movement out of the corner of his eye caught his attention. He swung the lenses and swore.

What were they doing there? The trio should've hiked to the construction site.

His jaw protested his clenched teeth.

They defied his planning and compromised his RV.

The metal binoculars bit into his palms. He wasn't worried about the cop breaking in and finding his identity. He had a fail-safe attached to the door that only he could deactivate. It was just his backup plan to leave wasn't the strongest, and he didn't want to rely on it.

Keep your eye on the prize. His father's saying rang in his mind. He could curse at the change in plan or adjust and take out the dog and cop from here.

Settling prone on the boulder, Julien ignored the crags digging into his front. Replacing the binoculars with the sniper rifle's scope, he zeroed the crosshairs on the RV.

Not much of a line of sight.

"You think you're safe." He clucked his tongue searching for a shot. "You're not."

He didn't worry about executing a cop. His father had taught him how to scrub a scene to erase traces of his existence. Once he had the treasure and everything Nicole owned, he'd blend back into his life in Chicago, leaving the police with an unsolvable mystery.

Troy peered through two healthy maple trunks and over dense mountain laurel shrubs.

"Anything?"

The scent of summer and earth wafted in the breeze just as ten fingers rested against the top of his shoulders. She pressed against his back and popped her head beside his.

Never in his life did he wish he could take a selfie more.

Barring that, he thanked God he wasn't taller. Normally,

he rued being less than six feet, but not anymore. He perfectly matched Nicole.

Waffles squirmed and pushed, bumping into Troy's
bruised and tender shin in his attempt to see through the
shrubs.

Doing his best to ignore the beautiful temptation behind
him, Troy scanned the RV. "Nothing. I haven't seen a cur-
tain twitch or the vehicle shift like someone moved inside."

They had crept along the tree line as close to the access
road as possible. Certain areas were too dense to navigate,
forcing them to move deeper into the forest, but this spot
wasn't bad. The vantage of the camper door, window, and
the back gave him enough to study.

"We going to check it out?"

Nicole's whisper tickled his ear as her breaths puffed
against his cheek.

Her question sank in. "Nope. *We* aren't going to do anything. *I'm* going—"

"Nope." Her fingers turned into claws. "We do this *together.*"

"Nicole," he growled.

"I'm vulnerable by myself."

He snapped his chin toward hers, catching the flash
of insecurity before she hid it behind a flimsy mask. She
should never play poker.

His gaze slipped to her lips. Centimeters from his.

She jerked away, putting space between their bodies.
"You need Waffles's senses. We're a package deal."

He didn't like it one bit, but didn't have a good argument against her statement. "Do everything I say. Got it?"

Thrusting her shoulders back, she nodded. "You're the
boss for the moment."

He rolled his eyes. "Had to add that last bit on."

"Yup."

"I go first." He stretched his neck left, then right. "Stay behind me and keep a tight leash on the dog."

He pushed through the bushes. Stones crunched beneath his boots the moment he stepped onto the road.

Waffles hustled beside him, then scratched his thigh, managing to catch beneath Troy's shorts.

"Ow, Waffles." Troy jerked away.

"Woof."

Dirt and gravel kicked up, flying off the road. Where he just stood.

Waffles headbutted him, knocking him sideways.

A second *thwack* sent more of the road scattering.

Without a conscious thought, Troy grabbed Nicole and ran toward the RV. "Sniper," he barked, calculating angles and trajectories. Shots were coming from somewhere higher and to the left.

Waffles tore ahead of them, helping to hustle Nicole out of the open area.

She flattened against the back, next to an anchored ladder leading to the roof, heaving air in and out.

He searched their surroundings.

They couldn't stay behind the RV. Psycho wouldn't remain in place long. They had to run back into the forest. Use the trees and boulders for cover.

"We can't use the access road," Nicole whispered, clamping onto the back of his T-shirt. "He'd see us too easily."

Troy weighed the risk of climbing the RV's ladder to get a better look. No more shots had been fired. Had the guy already moved? "We can also rule out going to the construction site."

"He'd expect us to run there." Nicole mirrored Troy's thoughts.

Troy peered around the side, heart pumping wildly in

his throat. Adrenaline heightened everything and made his movements harder to execute.

Something whizzed by his neck. He jerked back as pieces of gravel flipped upward again.

"Groooooowwwwwwwllllllll. Woofwoofwoofwoof." Spittle flew with the menace.

"Time to move." He gauged the open area. A lot more space than he'd like.

Nicole bunched his T-shirt.

He darted across the road diagonally, keeping the RV between them and a bullet's trajectory as best he could. Nicole stumbled, kicking his boot in her attempt to find a rhythm so close behind him. Any second he expected a bullet in the back. His nerve endings were fired up. Diving through the mountain maples and laurels crowding the edge of the access way, his skin burned with scraping leaves and branches.

"God," Nicole muttered, "help us, please."

"I wouldn't hold your breath." Troy dodged around a thick trunk. "He stuck you with me."

"Then He's listening."

Troy snorted and let it go. Trees were a help and hindrance. He needed them to act as shields, but he couldn't run as fast as he wanted with so many obstacles.

Waffles scurried under a fallen tree. Nicole scrabbled to free the leash from her wrist and hand. The space wasn't large enough for humans.

Troy whirled and gripped Nicole's hips. "Jump."

She did, and he used her momentum to lift her on top of the rotting bark. Her arms flung outward, balancing on the slippery surface, then she jumped to the other side.

Backing up, he ran, leaping at the last moment. His boot landed on slimy moss, almost sliding off. Stretching forward, he curled his fingertips into crevasses in the damp bark. Muscling upward, he swung his legs to the side like a criminal vaulting a fence. He'd never score style points, but it worked.

Nicole slipped her hand through the loop at the end of Waffles's leash, crouching. Troy hunkered by her side, inhaling, then exhaling to slow his pounding heart.

Once he stopped sounding like an injured moose, he rose to see over the tree.

Nothing out of place.

Waffles licked Troy's calf as Nicole vigorously scratched the dog's fur.

Birds resumed chattering and insects droned, trolling for mates.

"Troy," Nicole whispered, gently tugging the bottom of his shorts a few times.

He nodded to let her know he was listening, not taking his eyes off their surroundings.

"I was thinking." She rose to hover next to him. "We could escape in the RV. Your truck is toast but the RV looked fine. We might even find a phone or something to call in the cavalry."

Troy impulsively kissed her lips. Nothing passionate or planned, just expressing joy. "You read my mind."

Chapter Twenty-Two

Nicole beamed, unable to stop the goofy smile. "I need to read your mind more often."

Troy laughed softly, his expression free of tension.

Tucking his joy into the special vault in her mind, she ignored the warnings to keep the wall around her heart. For a few minutes, she wanted to laugh and be carefree. "Who knew a detective would be so amorous about stealing?"

"Commandeering," he corrected, shifting his focus to the forest beyond. "There's a difference. We're not taking it on a joyride, and we'll hand it over to authorities for processing."

"Way to justify our nefarious actions." Nicole stole a whiff of his masculine scent, then covered her inhale by patting Waffles's head.

"Nefarious," he repeated with a grin. "Look who's breaking out the big words."

"I managed to attend classes at college between a thriving social life." Exaggeration. She had friends and dated, but she couldn't say her social calendar thrived.

He side-eyed her. "I bet men are always clamoring for your attention."

"Sure they are." As long as she kept him away from the empty planner on her phone, he wouldn't know it'd been months since she had a date.

Peering over the dead trunk, she tried not to sneeze at the strong decay. Afternoon sun poked through the trees, nourishing the sea of shrubs and ferns. Birds flew and landed, squawking their displeasure at squirrels interrupting their perches.

Nothing screamed psycho in the area. "What's the plan?"

Tension crept back into his posture. "Follow me. If you can keep Waffles silent, it'd be a huge help."

She gripped the dog's leash until it bit into her palms. "Aye, aye, captain." The sarcastic response left her mouth without her permission. Nerves tended to do that to her.

He smirked. "Keep up the good work, sailor."

"Ha. Ha." She freed her wrist from Waffles's leash. "Don't get used to that kind of response. My ship is more of the cruise variety instead of destroyer."

"If your ship has waterslides and all-you-can-eat buffets, I'm down with it." He clamored on top of the fallen tree, then offered his hand.

Waffles crawled beneath the trunk.

"Don't forget the musical acts and duty-free stores." She jumped to help disperse her weight, then demolished ferns and ivy when she landed.

Falling into step behind him, she snatched Waffles's leash before the dog trotted too far ahead.

Troy set a pace that kept her from talking, which was just as well. She hadn't fully recovered from the other runs, and her organs quickly protested the activity.

Julien spared a glance at the industrial chain and padlock lying in the dirt. Raising his SIG Sauer, he edged closer, squinting to see inside the shaded utility shed.

Both doors were wide open, flapping intermittently with the breeze.

Something heavy thudded onto the concrete floor at the same time as a low curse.

Stopping at the bottom of the paved ramp, Julien set his sights on the lanky, early-twenties kid struggling to right a fallen air compressor.

The kid bumped into the built-in workbench, knocking

a set of wrenches on the floor. They pinged and clanged, scattering beneath shelves, an ATV, and the tall toolbox on wheels.

Colorful words poured from the kid's mouth as he strained with the compressor.

Julien didn't have time to waste on the weakling. Every second spent away from his perch, his chance to catch the cop, dog, and twit sniffing around his RV dwindled. Logic dictated the trio would try to steal his vehicle. They might break in, but the bomb had to be deactivated within fifteen seconds or…boom.

He didn't care about the cop or dog, but he didn't want to lose his equipment or Nicole. She wasn't vital to his success. He'd eventually figure the riddle out on his own, but she expedited the search.

Thwump. The kid finally had the air compressor in its rightful position. Panting hard, the guy leaned on the workbench and dropped his head.

"What are you doing here?" Julien steadied his aim.

The kid's chin snapped up, and he stumbled backward, tripping on a socket wrench. His ratty tennis shoe flew upward, slamming his back onto the four-wheeler.

Julien ground his teeth.

Scrambling to stand upright, the kid smacked into the air compressor, sending it wobbling.

"You have got to be kidding me," Julien barked. "Are you high? What is wrong with you?"

"Who—" the kid lunged to stop the compressor from toppling "—are you?"

"I won't ask you again." Julien's finger itched to touch the trigger. "Why are you here? This site is closed."

"I—I know." The kid swallowed hard. "I, uh…" He cleared his throat. "I left my, um…" His terrified gaze flicked to the toolbox. "I forgot something."

Julien didn't have time for this. "Anyone else with you?"

"No, sir." Another hard swallow. Sweat popped out on the young face. "I just…" His gaze slid to the toolbox again.

"Anyone know you're here?"

"No." His pupils flared. "I mean, yes. *Lots* of people." His Adam's apple bobbed. "They're all waiting for me."

Julien relaxed, a grin parting his lips. Screwing the silencer onto the end of his gun, he shook his head. "Didn't anyone ever tell you drugs can kill?"

Nicole's shoe kicked a stump hidden by vines and moss. *Owowwowwwowww.* Hopping, she clamped her lips closed to keep from yelling out loud. The same toes that kicked the jug found the stump.

Troy twisted, raising an eyebrow as if to ask, *Are you okay?*

Fine. She nodded, stepping gingerly. *Just being stupid,* she added, *and not paying attention.*

His lips quirked, then he faced forward.

Waffles trotted next to Troy, and she let him. The dog idolized the detective. She understood the draw.

The man navigated thick bushes and slid beneath limbs with fluid grace. Like a predator.

She shivered. Too much of her gravitated toward the hunter when that trait should repel her.

Sunlight glistened in a small clearing ahead. Tall trees formed a misshapen oval filled with low-growing vegetation and saplings. The beauty soothed the anxiety gripping her chest.

Troy stopped, not entering. He crouched, so she did the same. Waffles remained standing, ears pricked and head swiveling.

Forest life thrummed around them, drowning most everything out.

Motioning to the right, Troy rose and they began tromping in that direction. She hadn't realized how far they had run until now. Watching every step and carefully creep-ing back took *for-ev-ver.* She was not cut out to be a spy or one of those Special Forces operators. Her nerves were shot by the time the gravel access road appeared.

Standing beside Troy in the same spot as before, she swallowed around her pounding heart. The RV hadn't moved.

Troy invaded her space. Was he going to kiss her again? Wetting her chapped lips, she stilled. Instead, he breathed into her ear, "Stay here."

She poked his chest. "What did I tell you the last time?"

His beautiful blue eyes narrowed. "The psycho could be back in his sniper nest."

"So it's okay if *you* play dodge the bullets?" Her finger-tip jabbed his pec again. "No way."

"Yes." His chin jutted out. "You're more important—"

"Wrong answer," she hissed. "And utter nonsense."

A muscle in his jaw ticked.

Boring her gaze into him, she refused to back down. Did *she* want to play dodge the bullets? Uh, no. But did she want to be left alone for the psychopath to sneak up on her? Definitely not. And did the detective have anyone else to back him up? Nope. He had her. An ill-trained part-ner, sure, but never a liability. And *never* more important than him. She'd address that hogwash later.

The muscle ticked faster. "Fine," he finally snapped. "But the same rules as before apply."

He took off, and she did her best to keep up as they crossed the road to the back of the RV. Clutching the lad-der, she searched for evidence of bullets smacking into trees or gravel in their wake. Nothing.

Flattening her back against the ladder, she pressed a palm over her racing heart. *God, I will never complain about my job again. It's safe and uneventful.*

Waffles sniffed the back of the vehicle.

Troy peered down the driver's side length, then switched to check the passenger side.

Inhaling his scent as he passed, she shamelessly drew it through her nose, using the musk to chase away the fear.

Waffles pulled, his nose inches from the ground. "Can we…?" She motioned to the dog.

The detective's lips flattened. "Be careful."

Loosening the leash, Waffles strode around the corner, absorbing the scents. The nylon trembled in her grip. She'd never hear the bullet striking her.

Troy crept ahead, keeping next to the paneling. She tried to copy him but felt stupid. She didn't have the training or grace to pull it off, so she stopped mimicking and did her best to stay silent.

Twice Waffles inhaled, then sneezed. What did that mean? Should she alert Troy? The dog continued after his hero. Chewing on her dry lips, she remained quiet. The three of them eventually circled the RV. What Troy and Waffles learned, she didn't know. As for her, she accomplished zilch. No one was shot, so that was a bonus.

"The driver's door is locked." Troy crowded her against the ladder. The rungs bit into her spine. "And I didn't see the keys."

Not surprising. The man probably had them in his pocket. "Do you think we can break into the camper part and search for a phone? And maybe some water?"

"Yeah." He didn't wait. Waffles fell in step beside Troy with her inches behind. Without hesitating, Troy flung open the flimsy screen door. She caught it, maneuvering around the grimy frame. He jiggled the inner door's knob to no avail.

Locked. Her mouth whimpered at the missed chance for water.

Scanning the area again, Troy stepped onto the bottom

stair. Grabbing the doorframe, he lifted his right leg and slammed the bottom of his boot against the knob.

She jumped.

The door flew open.

"WOOF. WOOF. WOOF. WOOF. WOOF." Waffles bit the bottom of Troy's shorts hem. He tugged, growling at the same time.

Troy fell off the step.

Nicole sprang forward to catch the detective.

Waffles pivoted and leaped. Seventy-plus pounds slammed into her, knocking her backward. She had no time to brace. She hit the ground hard, her head bouncing.

"Run, Nicole," Troy shouted, scrambling to his feet. *"Run."*

Confusion froze her synapses.

Troy yanked her up by one arm. Her shoulder screamed in pain. Stumbling to her feet, she flailed her free arm to keep her balance as she ran—

A fireball erupted. Heat engulfed her body and tossed her in the air.

Chapter Twenty-Three

Lying on his stomach, Troy gasped. Time moved in slow motion, and he had trouble comprehending anything. Ringing in his ears drowned outside sounds, and he couldn't make it stop.

Ahead and to his right, Waffles awkwardly clamored to his paws. His big mouth moved, but Troy couldn't hear the howls or barks.

His heart lurched. Why...

Two yards away, Nicole lay tangled in a thicket of mountain maple bushes. On her back, her arms were flung wide, legs enmeshed in bending branches, and her eyes were closed.

"Ni..." he croaked, flinching at the tearing in his throat. "Ni...cole."

Could she hear him? Did he say her name out loud? The ringing drove him mad.

Thick gray smoke engulfed the area, the wind ushering it in different directions as it shifted. The stench of ash coated his tongue and nose. He barely made out the sound of fire crackling and snapping.

He tore his attention off Nicole and almost lost his bladder.

Orange and red flames danced among the trees, gobbling the forest like a holiday feast.

Time snapped back like a rubber band, slapping him with details and clearing the cobwebs. *Camper. Waffles. Detonation.*

He wheezed, squinting against the sweltering heat. The concussive wave blasted most of the vegetation between him and the blackened RV husk. Scattered debris burned, spreading the fire.

"Ni…cole."

Nothing.

Tears he couldn't afford leaked as furious terror grabbed hold. *God.* Unable to articulate his thoughts into words, he let his emotions pray for him. While God wasn't a genie granting wishes, the omniscient being *had* to protect innocents like Nicole and Waffles.

The ear ringing dimmed as the roar of flames invaded his hearing.

Waffles licked Nicole's cheek.

No reaction.

The dog pointed his snout in the air and howled.

No. Grief clogged Troy's throat. *God, no. No!*

"Ni-cole," he cried, his throat tearing.

Nothing.

No. Don't take her, he ordered God. *Don't You dare take her.*

Fingernails stabbed his palms. *She deserves to* live. *You hear me?* His forehead thunked onto a fist, anger dissolving with overwhelming grief. *Why?* Another sob burned his chest. *You had her touch my soul.* Tears coated his hand. *I knew I wasn't good enough to be close to her. To save her. To—*

A loud pop echoed, followed by an earth-shaking *thwump*.

Troy's gaze flew upward.

The top half of a maple tree, engulfed in flames, fell to the ground ten yards away.

Nicole shifted.

"Ruff. Ruff. Ruff." Waffles nudged Nicole with his nose.

"Ni-cole." Troy stopped breathing. Did she move on her own or had vibrations played tricks on his mind?

He willed her eyes to open. Willed her body to twitch.

To do *some*thing, *any*thing to show he hadn't imagined the movement. *You can't die. You hear me?*

Sweltering heat ratcheted. He was out of time. He had to move or be consumed.

Troy braced his hands against the ground and lifted. Blood oozed from various wounds thanks to flying shrapnel and debris in the explosion. Black spots enveloped his vision and he swayed, on the verge of collapsing. Instead, he vomited, his empty stomach pushing up bile and dry heaves.

Once the spasms finally subsided, he spat. His clothing had plenty of rips and tears, leaving enough to keep his dignity intact.

Nicole cried out, jolting.

Waffles jumped back, avoiding her toppling onto the ground.

Alive. Another sob wrenched from Troy's soul. *Thank You, God. Thank You.*

The fire was quickly turning into an inferno.

"We have to go," Troy croaked, barely able to talk around the emotions lumped in this throat.

She grappled to sit up, pain overtaking her expression.

"I'm…coming." Agony drilled into his skull with every movement. Staggering, he managed to stay upright. Feeling the back of his head, he cringed at the lump beneath his fingers.

The fire raged closer.

"Ni-cole." Troy aimed his feet in her direction, not quite hitting the mark.

Tears streaked her face as she clamped a hand onto Waffles's harness. The dog remained still as she used him to help her stand. Her ripped T-shirt exposed gashes and bruises, and he bet her back was even worse.

Thank You. Maybe it was time he worked on restoring his relationship with God.

He wove his way to Nicole's side. Shunting the stunning revelations of his growing feelings for her, he scrutinized her physique. The bushes appeared to have cushioned her fall, but she could still have internal bleeding.

"Come on." Nicole waved, the motion barely discernible.

None of them took the lead, just shuffled away from the growing blaze.

"Run," Troy breathed. "It hurts…but…we have…to move."

Nicole didn't respond verbally. Picking up the pace, she hustled faster south, tripping onto the access road.

He didn't want to use the road with Psycho still out there, but he didn't want to be surrounded by yummy kindling for the fire either. Lose-lose no matter what they did.

Game over if they didn't pick up the pace.

Waffles stumbled, knocking into Troy's thigh. Troy staggered, his concussed head lacking balance. Blinking away spots, he found the leash whipping between the dog's legs.

Nicole reached over and grabbed the leash clasp on the harness. It took two tries, but she unclipped it and dropped the nylon.

Troy was out of ideas. They couldn't stay on the road. They couldn't run into the forest. Nicole depended on him to keep her safe, and look what happened on his watch. He'd failed her just like his partner in Philadelphia. He couldn't keep jeopardizing the people counting on him to have their back. He was a jinx. A bad omen. A curse, risking others' lives with his presence. As much as his soul connected with Nicole, he had to walk away.

As soon as she was safe, he'd do the best thing for her and disappear from her life.

Chaos reigned in Nicole's head along with a dull ringing. Every muscle in her back shrieked, some louder than others.

Thick, ashy smoke clogged the air in long waves and scorched her lungs. Spasmodic coughs erupted from her throat, flecking blood onto her hand.

Heat whooshed against her back.

The wind kept shifting, driving the fire toward the abundant forest, shrubs, bushes, and plants.

"Ni-cole." Troy lurched toward her.

Waffles ran ahead.

Terror didn't help her bruised brain process internal and external data. All her instincts pushed her to run. Run harder. Run faster. Escape.

She was trying. And failing.

Fire cracked and popped. A sound she'd hear in her nightmares…if she survived.

Chapter Twenty-Four

Julien stumbled, slamming into a tree.

Above the canopy, fire and smoke plumed. From the direction of his RV.

Had Troy and that stupidly named dog breached the camper's door? He hoped so. If he had to lose all his equipment, the bomb had better serve a purpose other than keeping his identity safe.

Studying his handiwork, Julien wiped his dirty hands on his filthy jeans. The branches and shrubs camouflaged the dead kid from anyone walking by.

Crack. A slew of birds took to the air as the top of a flaming tree shot upward, then disappeared into the forest.

He cursed, marching toward the utility shed. He no longer had days to terrorize the riddle's answers out of Nicole. Even in this remote location, he had an hour at the most before someone alerted the fire department and cops.

Smoke crept higher, its ashy stench clogging his nose.

Coughing, he ran into the shed and shoved his backpack's straps over the ATV's handlebar. Time to move. Shifting winds spread fire. If he didn't flee, he'd find himself inside the blaze.

Backing the four-wheeler down the ramp, he sprayed debris and dirt as he raced away.

He had prey to hunt.

Troy itched to hang on to Nicole. He needed help. The synapses in his brain misfired, telling his feet to go one way when he needed them to go another.

The trees passed by in a blur, but he wasn't running very

fast. Information kept getting lost in the fog dousing his mind. If he didn't snap out of it, Nicole was going to pay the price. She counted on him to know what to do, but he didn't.

Run. That was the only consistent thought.

The psychopath wouldn't give up. By now, the guy figured out they triggered the bomb in the RV. Did he know they survived? Troy hoped not. He, Nicole, and Waffles needed as much time as possible to gain distance and a hiding place. If a hiding place existed in a burning forest.

The empty weight in his holster reminded him he didn't have his Beretta.

Great. His body didn't have the coordination for a hand-to-hand fight—if Psycho allowed it to go that far and didn't outright shoot Troy. Waffles might be okay to attack, but the dog had to protect Nicole above all else. And Nicole. His gaze slid to her. He didn't know the extent of her injuries. He hoped the bruises didn't mean internal bleeding or something just as serious. She didn't complain or utter a single word, but she couldn't hide the pain.

The gravel-and-dirt road curved to the left.

Crackling roared behind them, gaining inches for every foot they conquered.

Orange streaked out of the corner of his eyes.

Nicole cried out, staggering to the right, barely missing the branch on fire.

Troy lunged. The toe of his boot didn't lift high enough, tripping him. Gravel rushed up to meet him, and he could do nothing to stop his fall. As he slammed onto the road, every cell blitzed with pain.

"Troy," Nicole wheezed, stomping out the fire. *Please, God, help.*

Waffles reached Troy first, shoving his nose against Troy's splayed arm.

Nicole dropped next to Troy's prone body, grunting at the pain spiking through her knees.

"Detective." She brushed bits of debris off his cheek.

Eyes closed, he groaned.

"Woof." Waffles licked Troy's mouth.

Troy scrunched his nose and twisted his lips. "Not the… kiss I wanted."

Intense heat charged ahead of the fire edging closer.

"I can't pick you up." She tried to swallow, but her dry mouth had nothing inside.

Hacking, blood speckled her palm, but she ignored it. Ash burned in her lungs, threatening to shut the organs down.

Waffles nudged Troy with his muzzle. *"Woof."*

"I hear you…big guy." His eyelids fluttered, then stayed open. For too many heartbeats an eerie glaze blurred his blue irises. With a single blink, consciousness filled his expression.

A wall of heat washed over Troy's exposed skin, and he shuddered.

Fire. Fresh forest for fuel.

Pops and crackles raged, igniting his survival instinct. He had to find shelter for Nicole and Waffles.

Adrenaline goosed his synapses to work together. Rising to his feet, he stumbled, dizziness taking over.

Condensed smoke chased away the modicum of fresh air.

"Look." A hoarse whisper fluttered in the smoky breeze.

Staggering to turn, he followed Nicole's line of sight.

If he could weep, he would. On the other side of the curved road sat heavy-duty construction equipment. All abandoned as if the drivers ran away in the middle of the workday. They probably had.

A tree dozer, backhoe, and massive motor grader were

in various positions. Looked like the county was widening the access road. Maybe the retreat center spurred other development projects, or maybe it was something else. Either way, salvation.

"Can you drive?" Nicole pressed a hand near her liver.

Only one of the vehicles had a cab large enough to fit the three of them.

"Come on." With the fire breathing down their necks, he was about to become a motor grader prodigy. If his brain cooperated.

The immense machine sat in the middle of the road. Thirty-four feet long, eight feet wide, and eleven feet tall. Six extremely rugged, thickly treaded tires, as tall as his waist, moved the operator who sat in a glass-enclosed cab in the middle of the long grader. A twelve-foot blade was anchored just below the operator and scraped the gravel and dirt smooth. A second blade was attached to the front to smash debris or whatever out of the way.

They reached the side of the huge yellow-and-black machine his mind dubbed *The Stinger* for some reason. Delirium most likely. One of the glass doors—one was on each side of the cab—hadn't shut all the way and banged in the growing wind. Two-step ladders in black steel led the way in.

Nicole swung the door open, her face tightening. "Barely any room."

"We'll fit." They had no other option. "You first."

Without a word, she grabbed the handrails and hauled herself up. She shifted to the small area beside the single seat.

"Ruff." Waffles placed his front paws on the top rung. He tried to jump, but the angle was too steep. His back left paw lifted to the first rung, and he stopped. *"Woof. Woof. Woof."*

Mustering his strength, Troy lifted the back end of the dog, fighting nausea rolling up his throat. Waffles hustled inside and lay against the space beneath the seat, panting hard.

Troy followed the dog in, blinking against passing out. His concussion did *not* appreciate running, moving, climbing, or any activity in general. Dropping onto the cushion, he stretched his legs to fit over the dog, then turned the ignition key.

The motor rumbled to life, vibrating The Stinger. God bless the diligent operator or the supervisor who had to deal with a brand-new employee. Someone attacked every switch, lever, and handle with a label maker. Using the labels and manufacturer pictures, he had the middle blade lifted on its hydraulics to avoid drag and the air-conditioning pumping.

A wall of red and orange absorbing green vitality filled the glass. The fire continuously spread on both sides of the road.

Even with the air vents blasting on high, heat invaded the cab.

God. Troy closed his eyes to concentrate on the desperate prayer. *Please help me save Nicole and Waffles.* The maelstrom in his brain continued…yet, the dizzying fuzziness ebbed enough he could process the information from his senses.

The machine was so long and unwieldy, he drove in reverse for half a mile to avoid hitting the backhoe and tree dozer on either side of the road. The loud *beep-beep-beep* warning gave away their position. Hopefully the madman wasn't anywhere close.

Once he had clearance, he shoved The Stinger into gear. Thankful for the all-wheel-drive feature controlling six wheels at once, he turned the beast around, running over mountain laurel and small trees in his way.

Finally facing south, he took off. He maxed the engine at thirty-five miles per hour. With the gravel and dirt already spread, the ride was smoother.

"How?" Nicole hung on to the seat back.

He understood her question. "Thank Chase." Troy struggled to focus. "He had a construction phase." He paused to catch his breath. His abused lungs protested talking. "Dragged me to Diggerland in New Jersey."

Power steering and a steering wheel were beautiful things on this model.

"It's an amusement park." Troy did his best to stay on the road. "Real equipment."

Blinking away black spots, he scanned the inside for a phone. A five-by-five screen showed a live feed from behind thanks to a camera affixed to the top of the cab. A car-style radio was turned off, but nothing supported outbound communication. Maybe help was already on the way. He could only hope the workers' absence meant someone alerted first responders.

On the small dashboard, dials delineated elevation levels and pitch percentages, and...a gas tank approaching empty. He wanted to roar. Why didn't he think to check the fuel before they left? One of the other vehicles might've had a full tank—

A streak of blue and black flashed in the side mirrors mounted outside.

"Troy." Nicole slapped his seat.

Appearing like a nightmare in the smoke, Psycho raced toward them on a four-wheeler. He fumbled with a backpack resting on the gas tank, then pulled out a SIG Sauer, leveling it at the cab.

Chapter Twenty-Five

Abject terror erased the pain ripping through Nicole's body.

"Duck," Troy barked. "Brace."

She bent in the small space between the seat and the door.

Troy slammed on the brakes. The sudden momentum shift impelled her forward. Her hand shot out, plastering against the windshield to keep from falling on Waffles.

The huge yellow-and-black beast shuddered, almost skipping over the graded road.

In the rear camera screen, the psychopath dropped his arm with the gun and veered right. Another few inches and he'd have smacked into them.

"Brace," Troy uttered again.

She clamped onto the armrest and kept her other palm on the window.

The yellow beast shuddered and vibrated, this time trying to speed up. The construction vehicle was nothing like her Jeep. It didn't respond quickly or smoothly, but she wasn't complaining. Anything that escaped the fire deserved respect.

A blue-and-black streak roared up beside her.

"Troy." Her damaged lungs flared at the yell.

"Brace."

His new favorite word.

She tightened her grip just as he jerked the steering wheel. The yellow beast swerved, six wheels, almost as tall as the psychopath sitting on the ATV, responded, forcing the blue-and-black four-wheeler off the road.

Troy didn't let up. He drove the beast over the piles of

trees and destroyed vegetation lining the road caused by one of the equipment they left behind to widen the area.

Psychopath slammed on his brakes. He skidded into a turn, slapping the side of a particularly large stack. The beast couldn't hold a candle to the maneuverability of the ATV. While Troy could drive over the downed heaps, the ATV zipped through the spaces and popped back out on the road behind them.

Troy swerved to the left, and she fell against the seat, growling at the fresh round of pain. The reason for the shift loomed out the front window. A dump truck sat in the clearing with a huge wood chipper chute aimed toward its back.

They couldn't keep playing dodge. Psychopath was like a rabid fly buzzing around an elephant. Eventually the fly would land. And bite. The only thing they had in their favor was fresher air. Psychopath had a T-shirt tied over his nose and mouth while they had glass and air-conditioning to help filter the ash and smoke.

Was it too much to ask that Psychopath fainted from smoke inhalation? She guessed it was since the rabid fly kept coming.

In the rear camera screen, the ATV closed the distance. Behind it, a wall of fire blazed. Red, orange, and gray consumed the forest a few miles beyond.

God, please. We need You.

The ATV buzzed up the other side of the beast. Troy skewed toward the four-wheeler, running Psychopath off the road again.

Nicole lost her grip on the armrest. Her temple smacked a hinge for the glass door, and darkness eclipsed her mind.

"Nicole," Troy cried, blood tickling his lips from the effort.

Waffles yelped, doing his best to pull his hind legs, butt, and tail out from under her inert body.

Troy didn't know what to focus on. Nicole passing out, Waffles bashing his legs, or keeping The Stinger in motion.

Glass broke.

Flinching, he inadvertently jerked the wheel. The Stinger swerved, and he righted the beast.

Air whistled, and he found holes in both doors. One on each side from the bullet flying through the cab. If Nicole hadn't fallen, she'd have been shot. It barely missed him by inches.

This game of tag had gone on too long.

He had one advantage, and it was now or never. The fuel indicator made the decision even if the gunshot hadn't.

Yanking the wheel, he charged off the road, straight for the forest. Fallen stacks of trees and bushes lined the side, but he drove over them. A few smaller trunks caught on the middle blade, but he ignored them. They'd either fall away eventually or he'd worry about them when he had to. Right now, he had to incapacitate the four-wheeler.

Lowering the curved blade in the front of The Stinger, he rammed into anything in his path. Granted, he couldn't take out old, fat trees, but he could destroy saplings, younger trees, and bushes.

The Stinger couldn't go anywhere close to thirty-five miles per hour anymore, but he pressed it as far as he dared. The ATV dropped away, unable to stay beside them. The trees were Troy's best friends, throwing obstacles in Psycho's path. The trees were also his enemies, becoming obstacles he had to navigate so he didn't ram into a trunk he couldn't overcome.

The terrain made the trek rough. Beneath the layer of fallen leaves and debris were rocks, dips, and crevasses lying in wait. The tall wheels gave him clearance, but The Stinger's long length worked against him. An ATV could zip around a hindrance, but Troy had to ensure all thirty-four feet cleared before he could turn or weave.

He rumbled through vegetation like a freight train on a mission. His objectives were simple: immobilize Psycho and gain more distance from the fire. And keep conscious, find shelter, protect—

He stopped listing. It wasn't helping.

Blue and black flew past him on the right, weaving through trees, moving farther ahead.

Foreboding dulled the cobwebs. Troy raised the front blade. He could only go so high before he cut off his view, but he hoped it was enough.

High-pitched *pling, pling* echoed. Troy pictured the bullets striking the thick steel.

The Stinger's front wheels dropped into a larger crevasse. The middle blade dug into the earth, grinding his momentum to a halt. He eased off the gas and tried different levers to change the angle of the blade. After too many heartbeats, he found the right combination. With the blade shifting its angle, the mound of gathered dirt and detritus dropped into the chasm, freeing the vehicle. Plowing ahead, he counted on the four tires in the back to push The Stinger. They didn't let him down.

Free of the crevasse, he searched for a way to end the chase.

Psycho dashed closer but had to skid sideways to avoid a row of stumps Troy had no trouble running over. The ATV tore away to get in front again.

The gas light blinked. He'd run out of time. Troy rolled forward, lowering the front blade. He had one play left.

Troy aimed for a twenty-foot-tall oak tree.

The front blade rammed into the trunk, shuddering the entire vehicle. Troy's arms took the brunt of his weight, still holding the steering wheel.

Squinting through the darkness of almost fainting, he gave The Stinger more gas. The tree fought back by remaining in place.

Troy refused to give up.

The ATV whipped around a set of trees ahead charging straight toward The Stinger.

Troy continued pushing.

Psycho paused. His left hand let go of the handlebar, and he pulled the SIG Sauer from the back of his waistband. Raising the weapon, he aimed, using his right hand to control the gas.

The oak tree's roots gave up the fight.

The ATV sprayed leaves and dirt as the wheels dug for traction. Catching, they rocketed the four-wheeler forward.

Glass pocked and popped as bullets tore through the window. No rhyme or reason to the onslaught. The jagged terrain worked against Psycho's aim.

Troy hunched as low as possible. *Come on. Come on. Come on.* His knuckles were white on the steering wheel. *Fall.* He glared at the oak. *Drop. Drop.*

It did. One second it hesitated, and the next its weight lost to gravity. Cracking and tearing wood echoed as it plummeted to the ground.

Psycho tried to stop the ATV, but it was too late. The oak slammed into the earth, bouncing twice. The four-wheeler was no match for the strong branches. Psycho flew over the handlebars, smacking into another oak, crumpling into a heap.

To celebrate, Troy passed out.

Chapter Twenty-Six

Nicole groaned. Her eyes refused to open, and she gave up trying. What happened? Wetness coated her nose followed by bad breath.

What…?

The darkness began to recede.

A pounding headache began to expand.

"Ruff."

Her eyes popped wide. Waffles lay in front of her in a tight ball. He scraped his paw against her forearm, then licked her skin.

Like a video taken off pause, a mental collage of the RV exploding up to her passing out played on fast-forward.

Troy. Her gaze shot upward. "No."

He hung over the steering wheel, arms dangling down.

Fumbling with his wrist, she felt for a pulse. *Where is it? Where is—*

There. Her entire body exhaled.

What happened? How long had she been out? Where was the psychopath?

Adrenaline dumped into her bloodstream. She didn't hear an ATV. She heard…

Oh, Lord. Fire.

Move. Move. Move.

Primal instinct empowered her to stumble out of the cab. Heat swamped her—at least twenty degrees hotter than inside the beast. Thick, swirling smoke filled with ash and particles advanced in front of the fire. Her beloved Pocono Mountains were being consumed.

It took her muddled mind too long to interpret the oversize blob to her left was upturned roots. That didn't make sense. Did they hit the tree? Is that why the beast shut off? They stalled?

Staggering forward, she clutched her head. Her fingers encountered a knot. Concussion. That explained her throbbing headache and the urge to vomit.

A piece of blue cloth peeked through the smoke ahead. *"Woof. Woof. Woof. Woof."* Waffles studied the ground, then leaped out of the cab. He disappeared among the vast ferns, then popped up, trotting toward her.

She made it halfway to the blue cloth before her mind interpreted the meaning. The madman lay unmoving. Dead?

Waffles ran ahead and sniffed the body's entire length. *"Woof. Grrrrrrooooowwwwwl. Woof."*

Her mental bandwidth couldn't interpret the dog's meaning, and she didn't have time to try. It was up to her to find a place to hide. The mountains were filled with boulders and rock formations. The other entrance to the bootleggers' tunnel was out there. Anything deep enough to escape the inferno worked.

Needing a tree to help her turn, she trekked back toward the yellow beast. Realization wormed through the pain, showing just how much she wasn't thinking properly. She wouldn't have time to find shelter, come back for Troy and Psycho, then journey back to the shelter.

Standing next to the yellow beast, the two black steel steps seemed like a tower to mount. She couldn't climb them again.

"Troy." Her burning throat croaked the name.

Nothing. No twitch. No indication he heard.

"Troy," she tried again.

"Woof." Waffles placed two paws on a step. *"Woof. Woof. Woof."*

Stillness.

Panic surged. What was she going to do?

The crackle of the fire raged in the distance. They had to leave. Now.

"Hooooowwwwwl." Waffles tilted his snout up.

Nicole leaned into the cab and grabbed Troy's forearm. "Hey. Wake up. We gotta move."

Troy groaned.

Thank You, God. Relief mingled with the pain.

"Wake up." She held her breath.

"Ni...cole," he croaked, his eyelids fluttering open. As before, it took him too many heartbeats to regain comprehension.

"We—" She hacked flecks of blood and black junk into her palm. "Move."

Grimacing, he used everything he could reach to help him stand.

She hovered next to the ladder, ready to catch him—a joke, he'd squash her—while he staggered down the steps.

"We have to collect the psychopath." She pointed.

Troy grimaced, facing the black smoke rising above the yet-to-be-consumed trees. "Run or we'll..." He rubbed his heart. "...have to leave...him behind."

If the roles were reversed, she had no doubt the psychopath would let them die, but that didn't matter. She answered to God and her conscience, not quid pro quo.

Waffles led the charge toward the unconscious man.

Her erratic gait agitated her ribs, muscles, and concussion, causing flashing squiggles to mar her eyesight.

Troy surpassed her, his body lurching more diagonally than straight on. Mountain laurel flower petals fluttered into the growing wind after he sideswiped the bushes.

Waffles circled the crumpled figure, smashing ferns and ivy, sniffing every inch.

Troy paused, swaying. "Go through his pockets." He pointed at the psychopath. "Take everything."

"Where are you going?" Nicole managed to crouch without passing out.

"We can't carry him." Troy turned toward the downed tree. "I'm hoping the four-wheeler's still drivable."

Oppressive heat pressed against her from every side. They had minutes or they'd never run fast enough to escape the sparks igniting fresh trees and scrub.

Concentrating on the madman lying on his stomach, her skin rippled, rebelling against touching evil. If she stuck to clothing, the search was survivable. She snatched out the old bootleggers' map. The other pocket yielded nothing. She hoped for a wallet to finally give the psychopath a name but came up empty.

Rolling the deadweight over sapped energy, but she managed it. Sitting on her heels, her fingers curled into fists. They refused to move off her thighs. Nope. Troy could check the front pockets.

An engine roared to life.

"Ruff. Ruff. Ruff." Waffles ran toward Troy navigating an ATV with gouged and torn plastic fenders.

He eased the vehicle next to Psychopath and climbed off, leaving the engine running. "Find anything?"

"Only a map." She motioned to the body. "You get to check the front."

Troy dumped a backpack next to her. "See if anything's in there."

Waffles shoved his nose inside the main compartment.

She pushed the dog out of the way and dumped the contents onto the ground: two full gun magazines, a heavy-duty flashlight, batteries, emergency first-aid kit, water bottles, cellphone, keys on a ring, and a ziplock bag with energy bars and a small box of matches.

Gold mine.

Troy grunted, lifting the man beneath his armpits and hauling him onto the rack at the back of the ATV.

Nicole powered on the cellphone and blew out a breath. Locked and no signal bars. She dumped the energy bars into the backpack, then shoved the map, her uncle's riddle, and the cellphone into the ziplock bag. Better safe than sorry. Zipping everything into the large compartment, she tightened the straps. "Waffles."

The dog licked Nicole's face.

"Lift your paw." Sliding one of the straps on his right paw, she did the same with the left, then used the waist strap to anchor the bottom of the bag around the dog's chest. "Is that too heavy?"

"Woof." Waffles shook rigorously. The backpack moved with him but remained relatively in place.

A bladder-loosening pop resonated just as a flaming section of an oak sheared off, tumbling against a neighboring tree. Too close.

They had run out of time.

"Climb on." Troy motioned to the ATV.

Nicole used the dog to rise to her feet and shuffled forward. Troy had found bungee cords somewhere, maybe the storage compartment beneath the seat, and strapped the psychopath to the rack to keep him from falling off.

Smart, and it relieved Nicole of the burden of holding on to Troy and the psycho without toppling off on the first bump.

Troy climbed on in front of her. "Hang on."

Chapter Twenty-Seven

Troy checked on Waffles.

The dog ran beside them, intermittently dodging bushes and trees.

If the psychopath didn't hog the storage rack, Troy would've had Waffles save his energy.

The backpack sloshed with the dog's gait but didn't mar it. He commended Nicole's ingenuity. They needed the supplies, and she found the perfect solution.

His head throbbed and his vision blurred more often than not. The ATV had amazing agility, but Troy didn't dare utilize the capability to its fullest. Too many trees and undergrowth blended together in his wonky eyesight. He didn't see double, but he didn't see clearly either.

Gray smoke permeated everything, dampening his view. Ash and small particles slapped against him, burning his throat and lungs with every inhale.

Coughing, he let off the gas. Foreign objects choked his airways, triggering his gag reflex.

"Troy." Nicole bent next to him, her face alarmingly white.

"Woof. Woof. Woof." Waffles headbutted Troy's calf, panting hard with his tongue out.

Phlegm hit the back of Troy's throat and he spit, the saliva dangerously black.

The fire was gaining speed. He had to drive faster.

"Take this." She shoved a water bottle under his nose.

He blinked at it. When had she climbed off the ATV?

"Can't." He straightened. "We can't stop."

"Waffles needs it." She uncapped a second bottle and

tipped it. A stream trickled out, and the dog greedily lapped at it with his tongue.

Troy grunted and opened the bottle. His organs wept the second the water slid down his scorched throat. Forcing himself to stop, he shoved the bottle at Nicole. "Drink."

Nicole tossed the empty bottle Waffles consumed into the backpack, then held out three energy bars. He took two while she grabbed his half-finished water. She lifted her head and gulped the rest, while Troy consumed the food in three large bites and fed Waffles the other bar. The moment the trash was secured in the backpack, they took off again.

The water and protein didn't heal Troy, but his senses weren't as muddled.

Crack. Pop. The fire roared like a freight train spurring him to ignore the risks. Giving the ATV gas, he squinted against the wind messing with his vision.

Branches from maples, oaks, pines, and other trees reached into the crowded space filled with bushes and plants. He wended the ATV as best he could. His battered arms were filling with scrapes and bruises from the times he couldn't avoid hitting them.

Nicole rested her cheek against his shoulder and hugged his waist. She didn't say a word, but her tightening holds and whimpers showcased her pain.

Twisting his wrist, he fed the ATV fuel. They had to find shelter.

Darkness held Julien one moment, the next awareness flooded his senses.

Something vibrated beneath his back—

His legs flew upward as a jolt rocked through the rest of him.

What…?

Cranking his neck, it took him too many seconds to

understand the forest whizzed past him. Turning to gaze the other direction, he blinked.

Why?

Nicole clung to the cop as the man navigated the ATV Julien had stolen.

The overwhelming stench of burning wood irritated his nose and coated his mouth.

Then reality swarmed back in.

Julien snapped his gaze behind him. Black smoke and multicolored flames raged in the distance.

The ATV jerked. The back of his head smacked against the plastic fender.

Why didn't he fall off?

Wiggling didn't produce much movement. Jamming his chin against his chest, he understood why. The cop had strapped him to the rack with bungee cords.

How noble. And stupid.

The cop should've left Julien behind. All he did was give Julien another chance to take the treasure and kill them all. No loose ends meant no one to positively identify Julien.

He grinned. The cop's absurd honorable heart was Julien's gain.

Wriggling his hand loose, he felt the length of the nearest cord.

Plink. The strap snapped free, dropping behind the ATV.

The second bungee was easier to unhook.

He detached the last bungee cord and sprang forward. Sweeping an arm around Nicole's waist, he snatched her off the ATV.

Nicole's scream cut off when she slammed onto a mass of Virginia creepers.

The world tilted and rolled, her head slapping the ground. Darkness encroached her vision.

Oomph. Her body jerked to a halt on her back.

Slamming her eyes closed, she fought the urge to gag.

Something heavy dropped onto her chest, constricting the air in her lungs.

Eyelids flying open, horror spurred her hips to buck in every direction. Her fists flailed, striking the psychopath, but having no effect.

Worming his arms through her fists, coarse skin clamped around her throat.

"No," she wheezed, convulsively swallowing. She jammed a palm beneath his chin and pushed. *No. No. God, no.*

As he jerked free of her palm, his black eyes burned into hers. "Stop or I'll crush your windpipe."

Instantly ceasing, her hips settled and her arms dropped wide to the ground.

Can't breathe. Her lungs screamed for air, and her brain seized with terror.

Satisfaction oozed in his ugly smile. "Give me the answers to the riddle."

She couldn't think. Couldn't process the words. Couldn't do anything but stare at the face of death.

"Nicole." Troy jumped off the ATV.

"Groooooowwwwwwwwwwwlllll. Woof. Woof. Woof." Waffles dug his large paws into the loam and dirt, turning on a dime.

Dizziness prevailed, Troy's brain unable to keep up with his actions. He landed on his knees. Crawling forward, he grabbed a mountain maple bush, using the twigs and branches to stand.

"Groooooowwwwwwwwwwwlllll. Woof. Woof. Woof."

Troy stumbled to the right, willing his mind to catch up. He had to get to Nicole.

"If you don't call off this dog," Psycho yelled, "I'll kill her."

Ripping his gaze off the unsteady ground, Troy locked

onto the hands encircling Nicole's throat. She lay unmoving beneath the psychopath. Defenseless.

Red hazed Troy's vision.

Menacing snarls rumbled from Waffles's chest, mirroring Troy's own. The dog stood a few feet from the madman with his head low and teeth exposed.

Never did Troy wish for his Beretta more than this moment. "If you don't take your hands off her, I'll release the dog." Stalemate.

Psycho tsked. "And risk harming your precious girlfriend? I don't think so."

"Waffles has excellent aim." Troy had no idea of the dog's capabilities outside of finding explosive materials, but he knew in his heart Waffles wouldn't hurt Nicole. They already bonded. Troy recognized the signs since he had done the same thing. With both of them.

"Groooooowwwwwwwwwwwllll."

Hatred poured from the dangerous man. "I. Will. Kill. Her."

Chills stole down Troy's spine. He believed the man would do it and not lose an ounce of sleep. "What's your plan?" He had to de-escalate the situation. "You're at a disadvantage. You lost your gun. How are you going to stop me or Waffles?" He motioned to the fire thundering closer. "Can you—"

Nicole's right fist launched off the ground and connected with Psycho's chin.

Waffles lunged, slamming his front paws on the man's chest, knocking him off her.

Troy closed the distance, his heart lodged in his throat.

Nicole rolled over, retching and gagging.

Waffles yelped and hopped to the side, avoiding a second kick.

Panting, Nicole heaved black gunk and bile. Red marks

in the shape of that…*man's* hands bloomed on her delicate skin.

Dropping next to her, branches and twigs dug into his exposed knees. The spikes of pain were nothing compared with the nightmare Nicole just experienced.

"I've got you." He situated her in his arms, cradling her like precious cargo. Waffles couldn't distract the psycho much longer. They had to run.

"Woof. Woof. Woof." Snarl. Waffles sprang toward the madman attempting to stand.

Troy balanced on the balls of his feet. He swayed, vertigo dominating his balance.

Nicole curled her swelling right hand against his chest, crying.

His heart splintered into pieces.

"I'm sorry." The apology came out thick and useless. She fought for her life because he failed to protect her again.

Muscling straight up, he took a step to keep from falling over. The world tilted and blackened from standing too fast.

Blinking to clear his sight, he loped for the ATV.

Nicole wheezed, turning into him and muffling her cries.

Leaning his butt against the four-wheeler's bench seat, he hugged Nicole and spun on his rear, throwing his right leg over. Ungraceful. Awkward. But effective.

He whistled for Waffles. Time to put distance between themselves, the fire, and Psycho.

Chapter Twenty-Eight

Julien punched the dirt.

Twice. Twice he'd been beaten by that cop.

No more. Shoving to his feet, he took off after the ATV. He had no hope of catching the four-wheeler, but that didn't stop him from following the tracks. The machine would eventually run out of gas. When it did, Julien would be waiting in the shadows to end this game of cat and mouse once and for all.

Nicole bunched Troy's shirt to keep from falling off. The ATV rumbled beneath her butt, her legs thrown over Troy's thigh with her shoes dangling and bobbing.

He tore through the forest, jerking the vehicle around obstacles. With her face pressed against his chest, she trusted him to not to kill—

A sob erupted.

Phantom hands squeezed her neck. They wouldn't stop. They kept tightening, and tightening…

She jerked, gasping for air.

Troy kissed the top of her head. "You're safe."

Her swallow scraped against her damaged larynx, shooting searing pain through her throat.

Close. She'd been so close to dying.

Another sob stole her air.

Sniper bullets. Gunfire in the dark. Exploding RV. All of those attempts were terrifying and horrific, but… Strangling. That was personal. Lying helpless beneath that psychopath—

Her breath caught.

The feel of his thighs clenching her ribs… She clamped her eyelids harder. *Stop.*

Coarse skin wrapping around her throat…

No. Tears soaked Troy's shirt.

Evil grinned down at her…

Make it stop.

The ATV veered to the right, then sharply left. The sinister face disappeared as she held on. Troy toed the four-wheeler into another gear. The revving engine drowned the fire sure to be raging close behind them. If only it would douse the memories.

Every knuckle on her right hand throbbed. Nailing that madman in the jaw wasn't enough, and almost wasn't in time.

The phantom hands continued to *squeeze.*

"Ruff. Ruff. Ruff."

The invisible grip slackened at Waffles's bark.

I can't do this. She shuddered, barely finding air. *God, I can't do this. I'm not strong enough. I can't handle any more. Please. No more. Take me home.*

Where was home? Her uncle's house? Once-cherished memories were tainted with a reality she barely accepted. Her former sterile apartment in Maryland? That had never been a home. Her mother's house? She didn't belong there.

Home might as well be Timbuktu. She belonged no-where.

"Woof. Ruffruffruff."

Except with Waffles. She cracked open her eyes. The dog ran alongside the vehicle, keeping pace.

"I've got you." Troy briefly stroked her back.

And maybe with Troy?

"Hang on." The muscles in his thigh hardened just as the ATV rocked.

Her arms tightened around his chest. Her swollen right hand had trouble maintaining her grip on his shirt. Once again, the detective pulled her out of danger. Her heart melted toward him, but her brain preached caution. Uncle Ross taught an excruciating lesson. She couldn't let herself fall in love with Detective Troy Hollenbeck until she knew what lurked beneath the surface.

The ATV's front right wheel lifted over something large. Clinging to Troy, she tilted with him and yelped when they almost tipped over.

Troy's chest rumbled, but she didn't hear what he muttered.

Adrenaline flared through her system, pounding her aching head and agitating her tenuous nerves. If she survived she was moving to the beach. This adventure cured her of mountain living. Forever.

"Cover your face."

Snapping her eyes shut, she buried her nose against her arm and his chest.

Cracking echoed in front of her. The engine muffled and groaned.

Troy's muscles engaged, each tendon working hard on something.

Stabbing scrapes on her shins and arm jerked her head from hiding.

A towering wall of overgrown mountain maple bushes covered in honeysuckle vines enveloped the ATV.

"Troy," she rasped, wincing at the fresh sticks and jabs.

"I know." His jaw muscle ticked. "It was this—" he manhandled the steering to remain straight "—or slam into oak trees."

The ATV shuddered, the engine sputtering and struggling.

With no warning, the four-wheeler shot forward. Smoke-filled light stabbed her eyes as the bushes gave way and tree canopy was no longer above.

Waffles yelped, baying from behind.

The sense of flying floated her stomach just as the ATV's engine died.

Strong arms clamped around her chest like a vise, squeezing too hard.

"Tight." She struggled to inhale.

Twisting violently, Troy wrenched them off the vehicle.

She had no time to brace, no time to scream. One moment she sat on the ATV, the next, her legs dropped straight, smacking into his. Air existed below her feet.

Before she could process why, her cross-trainers hit something hard.

Troy cradled her head and shoulders between his meaty arms, shoving her cheek against his sternum.

They smacked down hard, knocking them over. He landed first, inertia driving her body weight into him. The earth whirled as her shoulder blades to heels struck the ground. Troy morphed from a barnacle into a Zamboni, flattening her.

Flip. Flip. Squash. Flip. Flip. Squish.

Over and over they rolled. Bouncing occasionally to really accentuate the flattening times. Plants and debris took great joy in turning her into a pincushion. Rocks and other immovable surfaces added dents and bruises.

Momentum picked up, throwing them downward.

Nicole tried to thrust her legs out to stop their trek, but her heels only skipped over the dirt instead of digging in. She clawed and grasped, desperately trying to find anything to grab. The plants either ripped out of the ground or abraded her palms as they slipped through her fingers.

Troy continued to brace himself around her. Grunts and moans uttered, the bullheaded man taking on more pain than he should. Chivalry had its place. Tumbling down a mountain was not one of them. He could break a bone or knock himself out, then they'd both be in trouble.

"Let." *Oomph.* Rock to the liver. "Go."

Arms remained locked in place.

"Troy," she croaked, then gurgled at his weight splatting her. "Let go."

"No," he grunted, air sucking over his lips.

"Now." She pushed off his shoulders just as they flipped again. Momentum worked in her favor this time. He bounced off her, his hands grappling to resecure his grip, but his weight worked against him. It quickly took him out of reach.

She rolled after him, throwing her hips and legs downward to change her angle. She had to position herself vertically. The tops of her shoes stuttered over ferns and other low-growing plants. She managed to latch onto a Virginia creeper vine, still struggling to become perpendicular. It worked. Her velocity slowed, sliding her downward on her stomach, legs first, instead of rolling out of control. The vine stretched taut, vibrating as its roots slowly tore from the ground. The vine burrowed into her palms, exacerbating her injured hand. Digging her shoes into the dirt, she slipped another few inches.

No. Please. Her soles found a hard surface acting as a ledge, halting her descent.

As she heaved to replenish air into her abused lungs, her forehead thudded into a clump of thick moss.

Every concussion symptom roared to life. Nausea roiled and her damaged larynx wailed, her throat on fire. Had she screamed? Or tried to?

Bruises formed on top of bruises, and she dreaded standing up. Staying low to the ground sounded good to her.

Stop stalling. Open your eyes and find out just how bad your new situation is.

Lifting her head, she cracked open her eyelids.

Chapter Twenty-Nine

Troy clung to the limb protruding from stone. Wind buffeted him from all directions, loosening his tenuous hold.

Tilting his head back, piercing pain stabbed through his brain. His concussion wanted no parts of moving his head. Smoke obscured the sun, and the tree's branch shook with every sway of his dangling body.

Bark bit into his fingers, slicing little cuts. Blood seeped, and affected his ability to hang on.

Leaves tore from the stunted tree's other limbs, fluttering around him like snow. He twitched his nose to keep from sneezing. He couldn't afford any sharp movements.

Don't look down. The advice lasted all of ten seconds. Tucking his chin against his chest, he moved his gaze along the craggy stone wall five feet away. Striations cut into the rock face showcased multiple colors, including dark blues, grays, browns, and sparkles. It would be an amazing sight in the sunlight. Now? Not so much.

A dry ravine full of oversize boulders, hearty vegetation, and various species of trees rested approximately thirty feet below his boots. The blue-and-black four-wheeler had sailed over the edge and smashed against the boulders, throwing debris an impressive distance. He *might* survive a fall, but his bones would break for sure.

Deer, raccoons, rabbits, and other wild creatures ran, jumped, and crawled in the ravine. Birds squawked, flying in a cacophony of formations. All escaping the new predator stalking the forest: fire.

"Nicole." The name barely carried above the wind and

inferno raging just beyond his sight. Clearing his throat, he tried again. "Nicole."

The rolling and jostling had been too much to maintain his hold. Guilt and defeat weighted his limbs. He had tried so hard to protect her, but he'd failed in the end. The moment he'd been ripped away, his momentum accelerated. No amount of scrabbling for purchase slowed his descent. Only when he slammed into this squat willow tree's trunk did he stop. Sort of. He bounced and rolled beyond the edge of the steep slope and managed to grab onto his current branch instead of falling completely. The moment his blackened vision cleared, he searched for Nicole to no avail. Had she dropped over the edge and he'd missed her? Nothing resembling a human resided below.

Panic goosed his blood. Was she hurt? Had she broken something? Was she passed out? So many scenarios sprang into his fertile imagination, each more gruesome than the last. *No.* He had to find her. Make sure she was okay. Alarm tripled his pulse.

"Nicole," he yelled, or tried to. His throbbing head and smoke-damaged lungs only allowed so much volume.

Gravity worked against him. One hundred and seventy-three pounds of muscle and bone pulled on his shoulder sockets. His ligaments strained and squealed as the blood coating his fingers continued to loosen his grip.

Wood creaked, chilling his blood. Snapping his gaze up, he blinked black spots away. The stunted trunk shook. More leaves fluttered into the wind. Three willow trees had implanted in the dirt and stone on the edge of where the slope became almost a cliff. Their shallow roots allowed them to grow but not very large. Unfortunately, he'd grabbed onto the outer right tree. No other branches existed to help him climb. Only air buffeted his body, making things worse.

The limb creaked and dipped.

He'd run out of time. If he didn't find a way up, he'd plummet down.

His fingers slipped. The branch bowed.

It was now or never.

Ignoring the stabbing in his brain, he forced his right hand to let go. His body swayed to the left. Muscling upward, he regrabbed the branch, his palms now facing one another with the limb in between. With the fresh hold, he swung his legs forward. His boots slapped onto the stone face, and he shifted his weight to keep them there.

Not allowing his imagination to take over, he let his left hand let go and instantly regrabbed closer to the wall. He did the same with his right, leapfrogging his hands away from the thinner part of the branch. Once his fingers no longer touched, he walked his boots up the stone.

Constant creaking froze his blood, but he couldn't stop. He had to succeed or—

He cut off the wayward thoughts.

"Ruff. Ruff. Ruff."

Waffles.

Relief etched away some of the panic.

"Find Nicole," he grunted, needing the dog to protect her. They hadn't seen the last of the psychopath. The ATV had done an amazing job carrying them away from the madman and the fire, but they weren't free yet.

He lifted his feet off the wall and curled them over the branch until his heels brunted his weight. Shifting to lay on top of the limb took a lot of inept coordination. Twice he almost fell off completely, but he finally made it.

The trunk shook and dropped a few inches. The roots weren't strong enough or deep enough to hold him much longer.

Hanging on to a branch above him, he crouched on the trunk and scurried over the bark. Gauging the open space between him and the top of the slope, he let go and ran, jumping when his concussion-addled balance tilted the world.

Nicole scuttled in a graceless crabwalk, her feet toward the drop-off. The intensity of the slope prevented her from standing. Her butt occasionally grazed the ground and raked clumps of ivy and wild grass. She scampered as fast as she could, but it wasn't easy coordinating her palms and feet in the awkward position. This exercise went right up there with running. She loathed it with a passion.

"Ruff. Ruff. Ruff."

Her hand slipped sideways, tilting her off-balance. As she slapped her shoulder blade into a thicket of Virginia creepers, her hip found a rock. *Owwwwwwwwwwwww.*

"Woof. Ruff. Ruff."

Snapping her face upward, she found the dog gingerly walking diagonally down the steep slope. "Waffles."

The Swissador's brown eyes latched onto hers. *"Ruff. Ruff. Ruff. Ruff."*

The backpack had shifted, resting on the wrong side. Instead of helping to counter the steepness, it added weight the dog had to combat.

Above, a hole existed in the six-foot-tall wall of bushes and honeysuckle. She hoped they had lost the madman, but if he somehow found their trail, there was no way he was going to miss that huge clue to their whereabouts.

Orange and red flames danced with black and gray smoke in the distance. Cracks and pops echoed as the fire consumed more of the forest. Troy had driven them far enough away to escape the immediate threat, but they had to keep going. With all the underbrush and summer foliage, the fire had an abundance of fuel to spread and burn.

Troy. She searched every square inch of the edge. She couldn't find him. Helpless terror held her tight, whispering he'd tumbled over the drop-off. *No.* He couldn't be gone.

God, show me where he is. Please, keep him safe.

"Woof." Waffles switched and began diagonally walking in the other direction like a skier navigating a black-diamond slope. Now the backpack helped. His speed picked up, and he trotted, aiming for her.

"Come on," she rasped, wincing at using her larynx. The dog needed to reach her ASAP. She couldn't take another second not knowing what happened to Troy. Her mind showed her visions of him hanging on to a ledge of a cliff, or dangling from a tree, or—

Her eyelids squeezed shut. Or crumpled on a pile of rocks.

She couldn't take it. The edge of the slope gave no indication of what type of terrain lay below.

Troy couldn't be gone. *Come on, come on*, her mantra picked up where it left off.

It was her turn to save him. She couldn't, *wouldn't* fail.

Her right hand slipped off a clump of grass. Her bruised knuckles were swollen to the point they resembled a long lump. She'd never hit anyone before. In school, she'd been in verbal altercations, but nothing that escalated into a fight. If she survived, she was suing Hollywood. They made it seem like throwing a punch was nothing.

Waffles carefully padded to her side.

She buried her fingers into the fur at his shoulders and scratched. "Good dog."

Waffles licked her forehead.

Pulling away to keep him from consuming half the forest off her skin, she resettled into her crab position. "Do you—" she paused to grimace at the burn in her throat "—sense Troy?"

"Woof." Brown eyes gazed at her.

"Troy?" She tried again.

Waffles's tail swished, and his big head shifted left, then right.

Hope deflated. It had been a long shot. The dog hadn't been with her long enough to learn their names. If she survived, she'd remedy that.

Her list was growing. With her concussion and injuries, she'd be lucky to remember her name by the end let alone the new bucket list.

She lifted her butt and began the awkward scuttle.

"Hear?" she rasped, searching for the noise.

Waffles kept walking diagonally.

Creaking wood protested somewhere ahead. Three stumpy willow trees grew on the edge, their roots visible and spreading wide.

"Troy?" Her throat closed as fire lanced through it.

"Woof. Woof. Woof. Woof." Waffles turned as if on a switchback, continuing his diagonal trek downward.

Branches shook, their leaves carried off by the shifting wind.

A blond head appeared.

Before she could react, Troy weaved, then jumped.

Chapter Thirty

The edge of the slope dug into Troy's stomach, expelling the little bit of air in his diaphragm. The toes of his boots smacked the stone as his forearms and elbows scraped against the roots poking out of the ground.

Loud creaking and snapping from the willow that saved his life muffled his hearing.

Roots began rising from the wild grass and ivy.

Scrambling to find purchase with his boots, he threw his right arm forward, grasping at anything. The tree was going to go, and if he didn't move, it'd take him with it.

A colorful cross-trainer landed beside his hand.

His gaze whipped upward to find the owner pointing at her shoe.

"Take it."

Nicole didn't have to ask him twice. He latched on and used his left hand to push himself forward while he lifted his right knee over the edge.

Her leg muscles strained and trembled as she pulled backward.

His right knee dug into the ground, allowing him to raise his other leg. The second his left knee touched dirt, he let go of Nicole and crawled forward like a baby after a favorite toy.

Or in his case like a man escaping death…or a man ecstatic to find the woman burrowing into his soul alive.

More roots shot upward, crisscrossing with the other willows' lifelines.

Nicole crabwalked up the slope as if a grand prize was on the line.

Waffles barked and struggled to follow her.

Troy continued crawling, his palms and knees banging into everything they could find: rocks, plants, roots, twigs, sticks. All of it pricked and bruised.

Movemovemove. The mantra repeated, spurring him to crawl faster.

Crack. Wood snapped. Roots lashed like whips, striking his gut and thighs. The ground vibrated, and he lunged forward. Catching Waffles in the side, he held on to the dog, preventing the Swissador from toppling, then rolling over the edge.

Troy would never recover if something happened to the dog. He'd connected with the amazing animal as deeply as the dog's owner.

More rumbling invaded the slope. Too many roots broke free of the ground, unable to hold the willow any longer. Branches scraped against each other as the willow separated from the middle tree. Suddenly, the trunk broke loose, and the willow disappeared.

Thwump. It crashed to the ravine below.

"Ruffruffruff." Waffles wiggled and fought Troy's hold.

Troy barely dropped his arms when the dog shifted enough to attack Troy's face with his tongue and bad breath.

Laughing and dodging the persistent bath, Troy rolled onto his back and scratched the wriggling dog now on top of his chest. "I'm okay, big guy."

"Are…you?"

His gaze lasered onto Nicole pausing her crabwalk to sit by his shoulder. The red marks on her throat had darkened, accentuating a pair of thumbs.

Shame and fury washed through him. Pushing Waffles off him, he sat up. Her delicate neck should be cherished. Valued. Protected. That psychopath had dared to wrap his hands around one of the most vulnerable sections of her body. Had squeezed hard enough to leave bruises. Had almost crushed her windpipe. Had almost killed her.

Her eyes shifted toward the drop-off, hiding herself from Troy.

His heart howled at the distance. "Hey." He went to touch her chin but stopped when she flinched and jerked back. His fingers curled as he pushed aside the ache. "I'd never hurt you."

She nodded, but didn't meet his eyes.

Waffles inserted his big body between the two humans.

Nicole scratched near the dog's ear. "See—" she rubbed her larynx, her voice torn and raspy "—way down." Her free hand motioned toward the edge.

He got the hint. She needed space, and he'd give it to her. For now. "When I was hanging out?"

The lame joke didn't garner a smile.

Moving on. "This section of the slope—" he pointed in front of them "—sheared off." He figured it had happened in the last ten years or so by the way the willow trees grew and canted. They probably started out fine on the steep slope but lost part of their base when the land dropped away. "There's a way down. It's ugly, though."

"Waffles?" Gray eyes met Troy's over the dog's back. Grief and anguish haunted the once-lively irises. "Climb?" Her finger motioned downward.

"He'll have to." Troy scanned their surroundings. "There's nowhere else to go from here." He'd driven them to a dead end. Even if they crawled back up, they wouldn't have many options, unless running *toward* the fire counted.

Nicole lifted her hips, resuming her crab pose. Her lips thinned, and by the size of her right hand, she had to be in pain.

Waffles's back legs shuffled to angle his body diagonally.

Troy found a position that allowed him to scuttle with-

out tipping over. "This way." He began scampering, aware
their mini break ate into the lead he'd fostered with the
ATV. If they were to keep ahead of the fire, they had to
pick up the pace.

Nicole grunted. She had a few choice words on the tip
of her tongue dying to break loose. If she survived, she'd
never hike in a forest again. Especially if the trail included
scaling a just-shy-of-vertical section.

It's ugly, she silently repeated, unable to mutter out loud.
You got that right, Hollenbeck.

Glaring at the back of the detective's head, she willed
him to know her discontent.

Troy lifted Waffles off the uneven ledge that abruptly
ended. The three of them had been descending by finding
anything wide enough to balance on.

"I can feel you plotting my death, Witten." Troy set the
dog next to him on the stone protrusion. His arms flailed as
he worked to maintain his balance on the narrow offering.

"Good." Loose dirt flew into the wind, disturbed by
her cross-trainers.

"Harsh." His right hand clung to the wall as he lifted
his chin to grin at her. The only clean part of him left was
his teeth, which would've shone in the sun if smoke hadn't
blanketed the area.

She crouched, gripping the crags in the stone to keep
from falling. Between her concussion, aching ribs, damaged throat, and swollen hand, it was a wonder she'd made
it this far. Lowering her left foot, she felt around until rock
met her sole. Scampering to the uneven ledge Waffles just
vacated, she shuffled sideways toward Troy.

"Tell you what." The detective studied the wall to find
the next makeshift step. "Once we're at the bottom, I'll give
you a reward."

Her eyes narrowed. "What." Her throat raged. "Kind?"

If she survived, she was learning sign language. *Real* sign language, not crude signals flashed by rude drivers or in a game of charades.

A twinkle overtook the constant pain emanating from his eyes. "I'll let *you* pick."

"Deal." Possibilities channeled the inner maelstrom into something semi-productive. Following Troy's path, half-baked ideas flittered in her mind. Most she dismissed right away, but a few lingered, growing in detail. Heat warmed her cheeks at the alluring one returning no matter how many times she swiped at it.

"Ohhh," Troy drew out. "I *have* to know what's going on in that mind of yours." He wiggled his eyebrows. "Does it involve me?"

The blush spread, baking her skin. "Nope." The lie popped out. *No way* was she admitting she imagined him finishing what he started in the dark tunnel. That she wanted to experience his kiss.

"Liar." He laughed.

Resting her forehead against the stone, she groaned. *God, help me out here. Can You make him forget the last thirty seconds?*

"Ni-co-ole," Troy teased. "We're almost at the bottom. I have a few suggestions if you need help." A low chuckle infused more heat into her blush. "I think you'll like my ideas. I know I do."

Thanks for nothing. Lifting her chin, she bluffed through her embarrassment. "I'm good."

"Hmmmm." He hopped onto a boulder leaning against the wall. "How about I guess? See if we're on the same page."

"No." Definitely not. If he mentioned a kiss, her fair skin would give her away. What if she misread that moment? What if she had read the moment right, but he changed his mind? What if he had just been caught up in that moment but really didn't feel anything romantic toward her?

And what if he did want her? her practical brain countered. She had too much to handle right now. Her uncle had her reeling. He shook her foundation and had her questioning everything she thought she knew.

Her heart didn't care. It continued to pound for Troy, and her soul persisted in strengthening the connection growing between them.

Chapter Thirty-One

Troy lifted Nicole off the final boulder by her hips. Pulling her closer, he set her down but didn't let go. Faint scents of summer still lingered around her, easing the stench of smoke and burning wood.

They didn't have time to stop, but he couldn't make his hands relax. Her perfect height allowed him to gaze into her gorgeous gray eyes without cricking his neck. Too much had happened since he first met her, and she hadn't learned the art of masking the pain. He hoped she never learned. He'd had to develop it long ago, starting in the police academy. Once he was out on the streets, he'd perfected the impenetrable wall. But for reasons he didn't want to explore, he didn't hide anything now.

Her pupils widened and searched his face.

Well, he hid a few things. She didn't need to know about his growing feelings for her or the turmoil they presented. He didn't want her to see the doubt and fear dogging him. How every decision he made and every step he took held her life in the balance. How his failures relentlessly pursued him, reminding him he wasn't enough to save her.

Gentle caresses smoothed up his sore arms, her once-soft skin now coarse and abraded. Everywhere she touched left goose bumps in her wake. Her gaze held him captive, urging him to show her the parts he concealed. It begged him to confide in her, to unburden his soul, to share his internal pain.

I can't. He closed his eyes, breaking the connection. The temptation to open himself was too great. She already had too much to handle, and he refused to be another hard-ship she bore.

Her hands dropped away.

His eyelids flew open, catching the hurt and rejection before she wiped her expression. It pierced his heart.

"Woof. Woofwoofwoof."

"Waffles." Her chin jutted in the dog's direction.

He understood. The dog might've found something. Thanks to growing up with a twin, body language and cues morphed into words and impressions. Sometimes it came in handy, like now when she couldn't speak or when a criminal tried to lie. And sometimes it was an anvil exposing more than he wanted to know about a person. Evil rarely divulged anything he wanted to see.

On the plus side, despite her feeling rejected, her body language—leaning toward him, blushes, sneaking looks, etc.—proclaimed his attraction and connection wasn't one-sided. Amid the nightmare and torment, something as precious as potential love was amazing. And terrifying. And ill-timed.

Letting her go, he feigned nonchalance to cover for his tumultuous thoughts. "You going to keep me in suspense?" He added a full-tooth grin.

Confusion twitched her eyebrows.

"Your reward." He leaned closer. "Tell me what had you blushing. My mind's been imagining all kinds of things." It hadn't. Only one vision plagued him. The same one that had been gnawing since the tunnel. To kiss her.

As if on cue, her skin flared red again, the shade deeper than before.

A forest fire raged, a psychopath was still out there, they had no idea where to run, but he wouldn't trade this tiny slice of normality for anything.

"Woof."

Nicole straightened, and with a regality befitting a queen, she sidestepped around him.

"You're going to have to tell me some time," he taunted at her back. "Or maybe—" he began to follow "—you'll *show* me."

Her spine stiffened and he chuckled. He'd bet his next paycheck her blush was due to imagining them completing the kiss. If not, the vision took his mind off their dire circumstances for a few minutes.

Waffles had somehow wriggled between or scaled boulders taller than him. He stood on the other side with two paws on an oversize rock, his head just high enough to clear. Loud pants blew bad breath at them as his tongue hung out of the side.

Pop. Crack. Whoosh. Troy's gaze snapped toward the forest canopy starting twenty feet away. Within, a distance he couldn't calculate other than "too close," black smoke plumed, then spread. It fed into the gray haze already smothering them.

Playtime was over. They had to run.

Nicole pressed against the front of the boulder, lifting onto the balls of her feet. "What find?"

Troy mimicked her pose, his arm brushing against hers. He couldn't help it. She dampened the inner turmoil and grounded him.

"Woof. Woof." Waffles disappeared, leaving two wet paw prints behind.

"Waffles, come here," Troy ordered.

The dog reappeared, water dripping from his snout.

"Waf—"

"Shh." She held up a hand, canting her head. "Hear?"

"Yeah, the inferno—"

"No," she cut him off again. "Babbling."

Her eyebrows snapped down. She scrambled to climb the boulder.

Unable to watch her further scrape already damaged skin, he lifted her by her hips. She used her hands and knees to scale the top, then jumped to the other side.

His concussion still messed with his balance, and his shoulder sockets bleated from holding his weight. So it wasn't surprising his trip over the boulder resembled a newborn buffalo learning to walk.

"Woof. Woof. Woof." Waffles dipped his snout toward the narrow band of water and lapped the refreshment gurgling over rocks and past the boulders.

Troy's mouth twitched, his tongue longing to join the dog.

Nicole opened the compartment on the backpack and snatched out a ziplock bag.

His shoulders slumped. He wanted a water bottle and energy bar.

She removed a crumpled piece of paper, then attempted to smooth it against the boulder with no success.

Ross's riddle.

"Yes." She pointed at the first stanza.

He read over her shoulder, "'I babble and chatter. I dabble and lather. I have various moods. I cut and intrude. Do you know what I am?'"

"Babble."

His gaze slid to the water flowing near their feet. Water that had been diverted when the slope sheared off… "Cut and intrude."

It dawned on him at the same time she smiled.

"Stream." She jabbed the first clue. "Answer. Stream."

The wind pushed more smoke into their clearing. Ash and other particles burned his nostrils, and he hacked. Blood flecked his hands along with black gunk. "We have to go."

She nudged his arm. "Read."

"We don't have time." Urgency raced through his blood. The fire raged closer, blocking almost every sound.

Her finger smacked the paper on the second stanza.

"'The heavens and trees are nowhere in me. Whether high or low, I've wended and stowed. Do you know what I am?'" He snatched the riddle. "No I don't, and we can't stay here to figure it out."

"I think—" blood spattered her hand with her spasmodic cough "—I do. Read third."

He lifted the paper. "'My names are many and wide. I've been celebrated and denied. My light pales despite the sun's rays, yet Witten offers me praise. Do you know what I am?'"

She looked at him expectantly, her eyebrows raised.

"What? I read it. Let's go."

"Think."

"I don't know what your uncle praises." His skin itched from the nerves urging him to move.

"Think."

"Nicole." He wadded the riddle.

"Hooch Highway," she rasped, coughing. "Rotgut... Road."

"Moonshine?" He unfurled the paper. "'My light pales despite the sun's rays.'" His arm dropped. "The moon reflects the sun. Needs it to shine."

She nodded emphatically. "Moonshine. Uncle...loved it."

"Okay. Great. Can we go?"

Her brows snapped down in time with her lips frowning. "Second...stanza." More hacking had her bending over. "Cave or tunnel."

Despite the need to leave, his eyes flitted to the words. His mind whirled with possibilities, and he couldn't fault her logic. But... He continued thinking. "Are you saying your uncle hid the treasure in the moonshine cavern?"

She clapped and nodded.

"The one we already visited?"

She tapped the end of her nose as if they were playing charades and he guessed right.

"You're allowing your concussion to rule your thinking." He jammed the riddle back into the ziplock bag.

"We go."

"Yes." Troy jabbed a thumb in the opposite direction. "*That* way."

Red patches flared beneath the dirt on her cheeks. "No." She swallowed, grimacing.

The bruises on her neck were worsening along with all the others poking through her ripped clothing.

"Troy," she whispered, closing the distance until only inches remained. "We were…meant…to find—" she pulled out the aging folded paper "—this." She snapped it open.

The bootleggers' map the psychopath had in his back pocket.

"Other tunnel—" pause two seconds for pain "—entrance is somewhere."

"Nicole, you thought I was about to blow us up when I lit a match." He swiped her hair away from her temple. Dried blood coated the area. When had she gotten that? "Now you want to go back when the forest is on *fire*?"

"Yes." Her gray eyes implored him to listen. "Cavern. Tunnels…deep. Fire reach…area by now." Pain laced her eyes at swallowing. "No explosion."

Gripping her biceps he wanted to shake some sense into her. They needed to keep running until they found shelter. The fire department had to know about the inferno by now. The three of them just had to hang on long enough to be rescued.

"Safest place…for us."

The adrenaline in his blood impelled his feet to move. No more talking.

"My reward."

"What?" His gaze snapped from the tree line to hers.

"Reward," she repeated. "You said—"

"I thought you'd ask for juicy personal details or maybe a kiss." He jammed his hands into his matted hair.

"Kiss?"

Embarrassment warmed his cheeks. He hadn't meant to admit that out loud. "You were thinking about it, too." He pointed at her. "Don't lie."

"I was." Her shrug didn't quite pull off the nonchalance she strived for. "But I…want this." She shook the old paper. "Important. Safest place…for us."

His concussion was ruling *his* thinking. Underground shelter was exactly what he lobbied to find. And with the map, they had a chance of locating it.

"You win."

Chapter Thirty-Two

Nicole salivated and licked her bottom chapped lip. The coating only made the dryness worse.

Troy popped the last quarter of his energy bar into his mouth and swiped the crumbs from his fingers. Waffles sniffed the ground, looking for more. He'd finished his bar in two bites.

Her throat prevented her from eating anything. She could barely talk, and the water from the bottle she'd shared with Troy hurt too much to risk solid food.

"We agreed? Follow the stream." Troy tossed the empty wrapper into the backpack still strapped to Waffles. He had tried the cellphone again, but there was still no signal. Even if they didn't have the passcode to unlock the device, it would dial nine-one-one.

She studied the rudimentary landmarks on the map one last time. "Yes."

"Pray we don't get lost."

"I have." She dropped the paper inside the plastic bag, then tucked it into the backpack, closing the compartment. "Hope God listening."

Ash and other lung-clogging debris thickened the smoke. If they kept breathing it in, the damage could go as far as killing them. "Cover." She tapped her nose. "Filter."

Riiiiiipppp. He tore the bottom section of his T-shirt off.

She tried to do the same, but her muscles were too sore and tired.

He pushed her hands away. He unsheathed his knife and sliced. Her favorite souvenir T-shirt was now a midriff. Not that the Cape Hatteras Lighthouse garment could be salvaged. She'd be lucky if she kept her hair after this. The stylist might have to shave it off to free all the debris and knots.

The vivid bruises encasing her exposed skin were nasty colors of red, purple, and black. Barely a patch of white existed. The bottom edge of her sports bra covered some of it, but it also pressed against the tender area.

Troy cut a second band of cloth off his shirt, then soaked all of them in the stream. "Think Waffles will let us put one on him or will he bite?"

Nicole bit her abused lip. Good question. The dog needed it, but how did she communicate that? Fumbling with the heavy material, water soaked the remaining bit of her shirt. *Eiyeee. Cold.* Her stomach sucked in at the drips running down her skin.

Finally tying the covering around her face, she lifted the third piece off the boulder.

Waffles's brown eyes gazed at her.

"You need." She crouched and studied his snout. She had to make a pouch to allow him to breathe through his mouth.

With Troy's help, they tied the cloth in place. Waffles didn't like it, but he didn't shake or paw it off. Win.

"We've lingered too long." Troy stood, helping her to her feet.

He was right. They had a small window to reach the closest tunnel entrance before the fire consumed the area. Based on their best guestimate. She had faith God showed them the right way, that the water marking on the map wasn't a completely different stream/river.

She fell in step behind Troy and Waffles. It didn't take long for overgrown thickets and boulders to push them away from the water's edge.

The cavern was their only hope. They couldn't outrun

the inferno. The wilderness's untamed land disguised danger until it was too late. They'd already found one dead end in the form of a drop-off. Another could be anywhere, and with no hope of an exit. Old hunters' pits might trap them deep inside holes or root rot might afflict several trees and the wind could topple them over. On their heads.

Distraction. Her imagination was just getting started, and she had to derail it. "Kiss." The word pushed past her lips without permission.

Troy paused beside a forty-foot oak trunk—one of many towering trees crowding the area. "You asking for one?"

"No." She pointed at his chest. "You...reward." Her ability to express why he assumed she'd ask for the kiss fell short.

"Hopes dashed." He turned and continued marching up the incline.

Not only had the unruly vegetation kept them from an easy—like that existed in their condition—walk beside the stream, but the mountain also decided to throw in the StairMaster nightmare with the added bonus of constant tree/bush/boulder obstacles for fun. Her calves burned, trudging the never-ending angle. The three of them should be running, but her inability to make it more than three steps nixed the attempt.

Waffles trotted ahead, then took advantage of a hole a larger animal made in the tangled thickets. He disappeared toward the water.

Lucky dog. She envied Waffles's agility and resilience.

Resting her palms on her thighs, she bent forward to remain balanced with the level of steepness. *Dear God, have mercy.*

With every puff of air, her damaged larynx throbbed. Smoke inhalation caused her lungs to swell—

No. She couldn't let herself go down that rabbit hole. That way led to panic and freaking out.

Four squirrels raced across branches, hopping from one tree to the next. Their actions screamed alarm and panic instead of the usual playful disregard. More squirrels followed, all running from the fire.

Only the desperate headed toward an inferno—not counting firefighters, whom she desperately prayed she stumbled upon. The wind kept shifting, pushing the fire wider. Obviously, her ground perspective prevented her from seeing how far and deep the inferno gobbled the forest, but the roaring was hard to miss. As they traveled northwest—the retreat center was north—the smoke and ash thickened, and the temperature rose significantly. They were losing the race to reach the tunnel.

That Waffles stayed with her and Troy and not run as his instincts demanded was a testament to how quickly they bonded. He was trusting the humans to keep him safe. For that alone, she couldn't fail.

As they climbed deeper into the forest, the trickle of stream expanded into a river. Where they had started, the land shearing off from above had affected the course to the point it hadn't recovered yet, making it appear more like a creek. Now she prayed it kept broadening and deepening. That meant they interpreted the landmark on the map right.

"What I'm hearing you say…" Troy puffed, using mountain laurel shrubs to help him navigate the gradient. Delicate petals of white and pink fluttered in his wake. "…is that you want a kiss, too." His first finger tsked from his side. "So greedy demanding *two* rewards."

Ha! She glared at his back. If she could speak, she'd let him know only one of them was arrogant enough to assume that, and it wasn't her.

"If you're good—" he followed Waffles trotting around the base of two tree trunks twisted together "—I might consider it."

Now would be a great time to break out the sign language

she hadn't learned yet. The sarcastic retorts and witty responses pouring from her fingers would serve him right. He'd be in the dark, and she'd have the satisfaction of wiping the smugness from his taunts. A Halloween-esque cackle resounded in her head.

Yes, she definitely had to learn sign language if she survived. Maybe she'd find a college near the beach offering classes. On campus she could talk a law professor into helping her sue Hollywood for misleading fight scenes while teaching Waffles to recognize important human names. Survival Bucket List complete.

She had it all figured out.

Everything except escaping the burning forest.

"Overwhelmed?" The wind carried his cocky chuckle. "I understand. I get that reaction from a lot of women."

Ohhhhhhh. If she could pick something up, she'd bounce it off his head. Why was he being so pompous? Since she'd met him, he'd been charismatic, but in a warm, attractive way. The past haunting him doused part of his inner light, making him sometimes appear reserved and intense. He had teased, but never made fun of her. Now, she had to contend with a fatheaded—

It clicked. He needed a distraction, too. Baiting her was his way of staying out of his thoughts. Intuition told her his failure in Philadelphia was playing with his head. It was messing with his confidence and probably had him second-guessing everything.

She wanted to hug him tight. *He* didn't have to save *her*. *They* were partners. They'd work *together* to stay alive. She didn't have his police training, but she wasn't useless. Summers with her uncle taught her basic survival skills. Combining her capabilities with his gave them a strong foundation and helped offset the injuries plaguing them. The *long* list of injuries sabotaging their chances.

Focusing on the positive, they had a plan, a destination

that should keep them safe. At least for a little while. With only one bottle of water and a few energy bars left, they couldn't remain underground for long. But the cavern offered shelter from the immediate threat.

If only she could convey that message. A single word, grunts, and hand gestures didn't quite have the same impact.

"Grooooowwwwwwlllll."

The hair on the back of her neck rose at Waffles's snarl. Her stomach traveled south as her mind asked, what now?

Chapter Thirty-Three

Troy froze, snapping his gaze off the ferns, ivy, and other low-growing plants hiding the treacherous forest floor.

"Ruff. Ruff. Ruff. Ruff. Ruff."

The hair on Troy's arms rose as he searched for the dog. Menace filled Waffles's tone, warning he'd attack any second.

Troy's training kicked in hard. Adrenaline surged, urging his feet to run. Find the danger. Assess the situation. Negate the threat.

Where was Nicole?

A presence behind him had him whirling.

Nicole stopped, her hand inches from touching his shoulder.

Pivoting forward, he marched, his burning calves and thighs screaming at the increased pace. The brutal incline taxed his battered body and sapped his waning energy. If the mountain didn't level off soon, he wasn't sure they were going to find the tunnel entrance before the fire invaded the area.

"Woof. Grrooooowwwwllll. Woofwoofwoof."

"There," Nicole rasped.

Out of the corner of his eye, her left hand pointed toward the river. Adjusting his trajectory, he fumbled to maintain the awkward position forced on his body.

Patches of white peeked through the haze of gray. Bushes and tree trunks blocked too much of his view, but Waffles's coloring was distinctive enough to spot.

Troy burst through a pair of maple trees, then stopped cold. His heart leaped into his throat.

Twigs cracked and shrub branches snapped and jostled behind him. Terror prevented Troy from doing anything. His voice box shriveled, and the only thing he could do was stare. And tremble.

"Dear God," Nicole breathed next to him.

"Grrooooowwwwllll. Woof. Woof. Woof."

Waffles squared off with a *humongous* black bear. The cloth pouch they had created had fallen off—or he shook it off—and Waffles took advantage. Black lips drew back, baring sharp white teeth.

Living in the Poconos meant coexisting with bears. Before Troy lived in Philadelphia, he'd come from a small town nestled in the Poconos similar to Bell Edge. Random facts flitted in his mind. Black bears could run up to thirty-five miles per hour. Their sight was average, but their sense of smell was superior. They searched for easy food sources like garbage cans, tents, and unsecured vehicles. But this bear was probably escaping the fire. Alone. No baby bears in sight.

A blessing they desperately needed. They had a chance of escaping unharmed.

"Don't move," Troy ordered out of the side of his mouth.

"I know."

Twenty feet ahead, the four-hundred-pound beast held its ground. Lifting his dark head, the bear sniffed. Once. Twice—

It snapped its attention on Troy and Nicole.

Troy didn't dare breathe or blink. His muscles and organs morphed into ice, freezing him like a sculpture on display. *Please, please, please, please.* He didn't know what he prayed for or why he repeated the plea, but he couldn't stop.

A heavy snort resounded just as the dominant predator's fur rippled.

Troy's blood crystallized.

Waffles snarled, lowering his head.

The bear grunted, then stood upright.

Oh. Dear. God. Troy swallowed. Hard. The beast had to be six to seven feet tall. Deadly claws topped massive paws that shook and lifted.

"Rooooooooaaaaarrrrrrrr."

Birds screeched and bolted from trees, their flapping wings adding to the terrifying cacophony.

Darkness edged Troy's vision as his hindbrain demanded he run. Now. *Now.*

"Hey," Nicole rasped, attempting to yell. Snatching a dead limb from between fern leaves, she smacked it against the tree trunk. "Go. Away." Horrendous hacking followed her words, and she bent at the violence.

The bear cocked its head, its paws dangling as it studied Nicole.

"Woofwoofwoof." Waffles stepped closer.

Troy's muscles instantly thawed, and the primal instinct to save himself dimmed. Lessons taught around the campfire rushed in, freeing him from the paralyzing fear. Nicole was right. Waving arms, sticks, or backpacks and yelling usually drove bears away. Especially now. The bear didn't want to fight. It wanted to escape the unchecked marauder rampaging through the forest.

Finding another dead branch, he joined her in whacking the tree. "Go on." He waved his free hand.

Waffles didn't care if his foe was three times his size. He pressed forward, growling.

Snap. Crack. The top of a maple tree shot upward. Orange flames consumed the bark, curving back toward the earth. Back toward *them.*

"Rooooooooaaaaarrrrrrrr." The bear slammed onto all fours, rattling the bushes and trees. With an agility defying the beast's size, it crashed through the thickets lining the river.

Waffles's paws dug into the dead leaves and dirt, pivoting enough to chase the bear through the hole.

Troy tossed his branch and wrapped his arms around her waist. Yanking her off her feet, he blinked furiously to clear the blackness still encroaching his vision. They had to run. Hide. Leave. Find shelter. *Any*thing to escape the flames barreling downward.

Panic piloted his flight. He had no plan. No route in mind. Run. *Run. Run!*

Smashing through the rest of the damaged thickets caused by the bear, he didn't feel the broken branches or twigs scraping his skin.

Escape. Run. Fire.

Whomp. The earth rattled. An intense wave of heat crashed over him, knocking him forward. Into the river. Water splashed up his calves, combating the extreme temperature attempting to bake him.

His arms sprang open, letting Nicole go.

She fell. Her knees buckled, submersing her body.

"Sorry." His brain was in survival mode, lacking finesse and the ability to think straight.

Water sprayed and splattered as he pushed his body into the middle of the river spanning five yards across. Once he reached the center, he sank until his chin was just above the surface.

Crackle. Pop. Pop. Whoosh.

Flames thundered and howled, consuming everything within reach. In seconds, a raging inferno devoured where he, Nicole, and Waffles survived the standoff with a bear.

The fire had caught up to them, and they hadn't found the entrance to the tunnel.

Game over. No spare quarters to reset the board. No lifelines to save them.

He tried. He failed. Again.

Chapter Thirty-Four

Rocks twisted and wobbled when Nicole added her weight. Flat, round, and jagged stones covered the bottom in random configurations.

Following Troy to the middle was like walking through uncured cement. The current flowed in the opposite direction, and the water's density added resistance training. If she wanted this kind of workout, she'd join a water aerobics class. This activity was right up there with running and crabwalking on the Loathe List.

"Waffles," Troy shouted, cupping wet hands around his mouth in a makeshift megaphone.

A bark answered from the other side of the bank.

"Waffles, come." The river wiped off a layer of grime, highlighting vicious purple-and-black bruises on Troy's skin.

Flames rampaged on the right, warming the water. Not quite hot tub range but that wasn't too far into the future. Decaying trees exploded, throwing debris and ash into the suffocating air. Thick smoke oozed like sinister smog choking the forest of life.

The T-shirt tied to the back of her head helped but wasn't enough. Anything short of a full face mask hooked up to its own oxygen supply allowed miniscule particles and noxious fumes into her lungs.

Her overloaded senses wreaked havoc on her concussion. Amplified touch, smell, sight, taste, and hearing exhausted her bruised brain attempting to decipher the data and respond properly. Her synapses were confused and sluggish.

The first few moments in the water cooled her swollen

hand, but the rising temperature agitated it. She didn't regret hitting the psychopath. She'd do it again in a heartbeat if it saved her life, but she did regret not toughening up her knuckles through kickboxing or some other self-defense discipline.

If she survived, she was enrolling in a slew of protection classes.

The top half of her sole found the edge of a jagged rock. She added her weight, then flailed when the stone tumbled on its side. She plunged under, and her mouth automatically flew open in surprise. The cotton covering sucked against her nose and mouth, suffocating her. Panicking, she pushed off the bottom, pulling on the material as she broke through the surface.

Large hands gripped her forearms, preventing her from finding air.

No. She yanked and wiggled. *Can't breathe.*

"Stop."

The authoritative male tone broke through the horror.

She instantly ceased struggling but gagged and gasped, her eyelids flying open.

Troy's beautiful blues captured hers and held her prisoner. Before she could process his intent, he pulled the cover down.

Air swarmed in, coating her tongue with acrid burning fumes.

No. She jerked. Water splashed into her mouth. Gagging, she choked and hacked. Blood and black gunk disappeared with the current.

"Pull the covering back in place."

Her body spasmed, and she couldn't stop coughing.

Troy squeezed the excess water from the cloth, then wriggled it over her nose and mouth.

Wet, filtered air cooled the embers in her throat and lungs. "Thanks," she heaved, trying to control her reaction.

Pain stabbed through her brain, her misfiring synapses at war with the primal instinct to live.

"We have to move."

No argument from her.

Waffles dashed into the river. He swam toward them like a duck at home in a pond. The Labrador side of his genetics won when it came to water. And, most likely, his previous human introduced him to swimming.

Snap. Crackle. The fire continued to consume the thickets alongside the river. She used to love relaxing beside a fireplace with the embers popping and flames dancing. Not anymore. The sound was going to haunt her for life. If she survived.

Desperation added fuel to her limbs. Escape. Swim. *Go. Go. Go.* Ignoring the agony and dizziness, she ran as hard as she could. The current pushed against her. Rocks underfoot toppled and twisted.

A loud *pop* followed by a piercing squeal froze her blood. Two feet behind her, a flaming branch full of maple leaves crashed into the water. The fire sizzled where it contacted the water, but the rest of it kept burning.

Dear God. Dear God. Dear God. Panic stripped her ability to pray. To think. To plan.

Run. Move. Plunging her hands beneath the surface, she pushed off the bottom. Hand over hand, arm over arm, she stroked, attempting to swim.

Troy led the way, his masculine body slicing through the water.

Waffles paddled, his four legs churning to keep up. His snout angled upward, processing the filthy air. If only she had time to craft another pouch covering.

Pieces of red-glowing trees and shrubs shot in every direction like bullets. All around her the water sizzled and hissed. Agony sliced her left arm. She submerged it under the water, swiping away the two-inch missile.

Tears crowded her eyes, blending in with water hitting her face. She wasn't the strongest swimmer and judging by her failing pace, speed was not her forte either. The cloth mask was instrumental in filtering the toxic air, but it kept sticking to her skin. It blocked her nostrils and mouth, sending water into her lungs. The sensation of drowning overwhelmed her, and her petrified mind offered horrifying movie snippets of prisoners being waterboarded. With this experience, she now knew she'd say anything to make it stop.

Unbearable heat dogged her efforts to escape. With every foot she gained in the water, the fire achieved a foot and a half. If she didn't find a way to swim faster, the fire would quickly outpace her.

Ahead, the river narrowed, losing a yard or two as it curved to the right. At the crest of the left bank, four oak trees grew at twenty-degree angles, jutting their full canopies over the water. Boulders interrupted the river's flow, protruding from various spots.

Maples, oaks, and other species on the right combusted. Orange and red flames gobbled the fuel, spewing black smoke filled with ash and debris.

Blazing bits of the doomed trees shot like tiny cannon-balls.

No. Her strokes became more frantic. The oak canopies were too close to the right bank.

Move, move, move.

She couldn't outswim the burning bullets.

Smack. Smack. Smack. Little flares of death pelted the angled oaks. Lush leaves burst into flames, causing a chain reaction. The fire rushed through the rest of the canopies, moving onto the branches, then down the trunks. Unruly thickets bordering the trees didn't have a chance.

Surrounded. *God, help.*

She, Troy, and Waffles were trapped in the water with

no way out. No matter how hard she tried, her body didn't have the ability to swim faster. She couldn't outpace the velocity of the fire.

Her palm whacked a boulder jutting in the middle. Standing, she assessed the danger.

On both sides, the inferno raged. Nothing was safe. Even the water. Burning limbs and debris continued to bombard the surface.

Paralyzing terror shut her body down.

Thick smoke plumed upward and outward, pushed by the wind.

The stench—

"Nicole." Troy ripped her hand off the stone and yanked.

She tipped over, sinking beneath the surface. That snapped the paralysis. Shooting upward, she sputtered, fighting against the cloth blocking the air. She desperately wanted to take it off. Knew she'd die if she did. Although, she might die if she didn't.

"Don't give up." He let go and headed toward Waffles. She wasn't.

Troy paused in front of the dog, then lowered into the water. She didn't see what he was doing until Waffles angled oddly. The Swissador's paws rested on Troy's shoulders in a quasi-piggyback. The two of them began moving, Troy doing all the work.

God bless him.

She pushed off the rocky bottom to catch up. While she was tall enough to stand without drowning, Waffles constantly tread water. He had to be exhausted. Troy probably just saved the dog's life. Did he have any other tricks up his sleeve to liberate them from this horror?

Chapter Thirty-Five

Troy told Nicole not to give up, but he was really talking to himself. Surrounded by fire, he had nowhere to run. Nowhere to lead. Nowhere to go.

Cradling Waffles's back legs near his tail, Troy pushed through the water. It was like running through sludge. Without his hands, he couldn't swim.

Wind rushed over the fifteen-foot-wide river, causing little whitecaps and ripples. It shoved against him, impeding his steps.

Trudge. Trudge. Trudge. Cramps attacked his calves and thighs. He gritted his teeth and drove forward, fighting the accelerated current and battling the treacherous rocks lining the bottom. Running wasn't enough. He was losing to the inferno. Waffles's added weight didn't help, but he'd hold on to the dog until his dying breath.

A two-foot burning branch with leaves smacked the water beside him. *Hissssssss.* It dashed downstream.

Fire escalated on his left and right. The underbrush and healthy trees gave it plenty of sources to spread. Brilliant orange flames burned into his irises. White spots marred his vision, creating glowing shapes when he closed his lids.

Adding to his misery, the smoke irritated his eyes. They constantly stung and watered. With the wind driving thick toxic fumes and ash everywhere, he had no way to escape the torment.

Squeezing his eyelids closed did nothing to ease the searing sting.

"Woof." Waffles's paws dug into his shoulders.

"I've got you." He adjusted the squirming dog.

Sweat rained over his skin in rivulets. The temperature had risen. Significantly. He'd never been a fan of hot tubs, and this venture didn't help. The longer they stayed in the water, the higher the chance they'd burn. Boil? Whatever the proper term for doom, it ended the same way. They couldn't climb out. Couldn't move closer to the boulders and trees lining the banks due to the immense heat.

He needed a miracle. *God*—he lifted his face skyward—*please. We need You.* The prayer didn't come easy, and it felt awkward, but now wasn't the time to withhold faith. Troy might not be worth saving, but God had to help Nicole and Waffles. Innocents needed protection. In the real world, good didn't always triumph over evil. In fact, he'd seen too many times when it didn't. But, Nicole and Waffles were the epitome of souls deserving God's aid.

Waffles squirmed and pushed against Troy's back. *"Woof. Woof."*

The dog's nails scraped against an extremely tender spot. Troy jerked, his left arm letting go to clutch the area. Waffles jumped. A wave of water slapped Troy's face.

"Troy," Nicole rasped, then hacked.

His attention shifted from Waffles swimming ahead to Nicole leaning one arm against a boulder. Her other hand fought with the cloth covering her mouth and nose. Blood spotted the material, seizing his heart.

"Nicole." He dashed toward her. The current slammed into his abused side as he slogged to the center of the river. When he had gotten off course, he couldn't recall. His mind wasn't working right anymore.

"Hey." He bent to see her face. "Are you okay?" Dumb question.

She shook her head. The gagging wouldn't stop.

They had to find the entrance. Now. His gaze swung wildly. Blurry vision refused to sharpen, blending their surroundings like a twisted kaleidoscope.

This couldn't be the end.

Nicole's fingernails dug into his forearm. More blood dotted the covering.

No. His heart slammed against his rib cage. No. Not like this.

The bootleggers' map had a crude drawing of a waterfall. If they found that, they had gone too far. He hadn't seen a cliff wall that could host a waterfall…had he? Doubt assaulted him. With all the pollution, the rock face could be two feet away, and he wouldn't know it.

Ash and particles tickled his throat and singed his lungs. His body bent as it choked and gagged. Imitating Nicole, he pulled on the covering clinging to his nose and mouth.

This couldn't be the end. Not like this.

No matter how hard he tried to inhale, nowhere near enough air filled his desperate lungs. Foreign particles agitated his organs, making him cough deeper.

Lifting the cloth, he cleared his mouth, unsurprised to see blood mingling with black gunk.

He laced his fingers with Nicole's, unable to speak. She stumbled against him, her body still in the throes of heaving. He managed to stay on his feet, barely. She found her balance and they slogged through the current side by side.

Step by slow step they progressed, enveloped by mind-melting heat.

Troy bent his knees to keep his shoulders below the surface. Occasionally he sank fully to relieve the intensity—not that the water was much cooler. His vision remained blurry, no longer clearing for even a second. Fighting the river's current sapped his waning strength, and it became harder to imagine escaping this nightmare.

The toe of his boot rammed against an unmovable object. *Owwwwww.* His nose smacked something hard. Tears instantly coated his eyes from the pain, blending blobby shades of green with dark gray. Wet clumps of moss dislodged with his exploring fingers. The rough and slimy surface stretched beyond his reach. Wall?

"No." Nicole untangled their hands. "No." Her forehead thumped against lichen and stone taller than her. *"No."* The side of her fist pounded it.

Lifting his gaze made him dizzy. Transferring his weight to flattened palms, he rapidly blinked. It didn't clear the blurriness. Up and up and up his eyes traveled.

Black and gray smoke obscured his view, preventing him from seeing more than a foot or two in any direction.

The inferno thundered, the tone different from before.

"Can't…end…here." Nicole hit the stone again.

He swallowed hard. Dead end. They'd fought to survive only to find death.

"No." Nicole pushed off the wall. Keeping a hand on the surface, she marched parallel.

Anguish converted Troy's boots into cement blocks, holding his feet in place. The compulsion to keep her close motivated him to move.

Large rocks hampered their trek, and the infernal wall refused to give way. Refused to let them pass. Refused to set them free. It kept them trapped. Corralled.

Smoke of varying colors became denser, veiling everything. The thundering turned into a roar, vibrating his bones.

Little droplets smacked his face in the swirling wind.

Droplets? He wiped his forehead.

Mist. *Mist*, not smoke. His fingers swiped at the confetti of moisture. As he reached forward, a continuous heavy weight hit his palm and spilled over.

"Waterfall." Nicole solved the mystery his sluggish mind couldn't piece together.

Elation swept through him at identifying a landmark on the map.

Despair shattered the joy. They had gone too far. The entrance to the tunnel was somewhere behind them. Somewhere in the flames. Out of reach.

No way forward. No way back.

Sorrow punched a hole in his heart. He had utterly failed Nicole. She counted on him to keep her safe, and he had done the opposite.

Covering his face, he fought the rising sob. *I'm sorry.*

The lump refused to let the words pass. His decisions killed this amazing woman. She'd die because he excelled at failing when it mattered most.

Coarse fingers gently peeled his hands away.

Dipping his chin, he closed his eyes. He couldn't bear the condemnation surely pouring from her expression. She had every right to blame him. To hate him. To wish their paths had never crossed.

Tears spilled from the corners of his eyes. "I'm sorry." The whispered apology was an insult. It didn't convey the level of grief eating his soul. He sentenced her to a slow, agonizing death.

"Nothing," she rasped, her palms clutching his biceps, "to be...sorry for."

The sob he tried to hide burst out. Her kindness slayed him. "I'm sorry." So many other words *needed* to be said, but only those two made it past his lips.

"No." She hugged him.

Keeping his body stiff, he didn't accept her compassion. He didn't deserve the comfort. The warmth. The forgiveness. "I killed us. Killed *you*." The dam inside broke.

Dear God, I'm sorry. His shoulders wracked, and he couldn't stop the onslaught. "I lead you to a dead end. I killed you." The words slurred and jammed together between heaving breaths.

"No." She jerked back, her eyes overflowing with tears. Desolation and fear resonated.

It destroyed him. He could fall in love with this woman

if he had the chance. Maybe he already had. Now he'd never know. Their time left was measured in minutes, not years.

"We're…partners." She motioned between the two of them. "*We* decided…" Hacking overtook her body.

The relentless heat and smoke became unbearable. How long would they last? No amount of waterfall mist combated the inferno overpowering the forest.

A storybook future with Nicole flashed in fast-forward, shattering his heart. He wanted what would never come true. Her and Waffles—

"Waffles." He hadn't seen the dog since he jumped off Troy's back. "Where's Waffles?" Terror mingled with sorrow.

Nicole stiffened, her skin paling.

He snapped his gaze everywhere, but the smoke and mist prevented him from seeing anything.

She clutched Troy's forearm, turning her body as she searched. "See…him?"

"No." The answer ripped from his raw throat. Had the fire trapped the dog beyond their reach? It was too horrifying to contemplate.

Her fingers turned to claws. "Waffles," she wheezed.

Cupping his hands around his mouth, he shouted, "Waffles."

She cocked her head. "Hear?"

He strained to listen. At first, nothing changed, then he heard it. Faint hacking sputtered within the thundering.

Chapter Thirty-Six

~~~~~~

Desperation ruled Nicole. Waffles needed help, and she couldn't locate him. Momma-bear instincts roared to life. She'd find her child and…and deal with "and" after that.

The mist was too thick and the water droplets too numerous to see anything clearly—her sight was already trashed due to the smoke. Keeping one hand on the rock face, she straightened the other. Swishing it this way and that, she used it like a divining rod or a blind man's cane.

"Waffles," Troy shouted.

"Ruff. Ruff."

Lowering her probing arm, she weaved to the left—

Whack. The back of her hand found a boulder. Shaking the sting away, she pushed against the river to step forward. The current before had been punishing, but now it was ridiculous. The waterfall created a force that insisted on taking her feet out from under her.

The crashing water from an unknown number of yards above deafened. On another day she might've reveled in discovering the wonder. She would've taken photographs and climbed/inspected every nook and cranny. Now, she just wanted to know if it swallowed her dog.

Gaining another foot in the fight to press forward, she trusted Troy to hold her upright. Clasping his hand, she molded it to her hip. His arm muscles rippled as if surprised, then he squeezed twice. She'd interpret that as he understood she needed help standing.

"I've got you," he stated—yelled—next to her ear.

Her eyeballs almost popped out of her head from the volume. *Ye-ouch.*

Rubbing her throbbing forehead, she inhaled, grumbling at the stupid cloth still trying to suffocate her. Through cracked eyes, she strained to see ahead.

One second nothing, the next something large loomed.

Yelping, she tried to step back but smacked into Troy. He didn't move quickly enough.

The shadowy thing lunged forward.

She threw her arm up to protect her face.

Two paws furrowed into her chest, nails trying to meld her shirt with her skin.

Owwwwwwww. Unable to stand under the weight, she tipped backward. Troy tried to maintain his stance, but suddenly, the presence against her back was gone. His hand hadn't disengaged from her hip. The mysterious beast pushed, Troy pulled. Her feet flew upward.

Splash. She sank underwater. Troy cushioned her fall. The weight on her front disappeared.

Scrabbling for a handhold, her fingers dug into rock crags. Pulling herself up, she swam forward. Right into the waterfall. A cascade smashed over her aching head.

Jerking sideways, she rose, sputtering.

"*Ruff. Ruff.*"

The barking echoed.

"Waffles." Nicole smashed the heels of her palms against her wet eye sockets. Her disastrous hair plastered to her cheeks and itched her neck. Wait. Lowering her hands, she blinked.

"*Ruff. Ruffruff.*"

Cool air attacked her skin, and she shivered. After the insane heat, the temperature difference raised goose bumps. Goose bumps she could see…without smoke, ash, or burning debris impeding her vision.

What?

Bits of spray hit her body, but the deluge…was on her left. What? What?

Her body was still in the river. She looked down. Yep. Still in the water, but…

Holy wow. Glowing orange and red distorted and swirled, showcasing the waterfall as if colored spotlights were on the other side. The cascade was so wide, it completely hid the river continuing to flow *into* the mountain.

"Nicole," Troy shouted. "Nicole." His tone became more frantic. "Where are you?"

"Behind—" she hacked, fighting her damaged larynx "—waterfall."

"Nicole." The cry was desperate. "No. No. God, *no*." Loud splashes somehow reverberated through the thundering water.

He couldn't hear her. She couldn't yell.

Marching forward was a lot easier on this side. Moving with the current helped. Bracing for the powerful torrent, she slammed her eyes closed and walked through the cascade. It knocked her down.

Plunging underwater again, she grumbled. If she survived with *one* speck of skin undamaged, it would be a miracle.

Miracle. Joy flushed the grief and despair, leaving her shaking and giddy. *Thank You, God.* He provided in their most desperate hour. They weren't trapped. They had a way to escape the fire.

The moment the rumbling against her body lessened, she pushed upward.

Right next to Troy.

His eyes were wild, and his body radiated desperation. He flung his arms around her, lifting. "Where did you go?" His racing heart pounded against her. "You disappeared. Gone. I couldn't find you. I thought you—"

Coughing, she swatted his back. She couldn't breathe. He squeezed too hard.

His grip instantly lightened, but his rambling didn't.

"We stay together. It's going to end. I know, I'm sorry. It's—"

"Not end." She arched back enough to flash him a full-tooth smile.

He stilled. "Nicole?" So many emotions filled those two syllables. The two that hit her hardest were desolation and hope. They visibly warred, tearing this incredible man apart. The man who insisted on blaming himself for circumstances beyond his control. The man who was far from a failure. She never would've survived without him. And Waffles. They were God's blessings. She'd convince him of that soon. But not now. She couldn't take roasting another second.

"Down." Single words didn't convey everything bursting to share with him.

It took him another ten seconds to comply. Not that he broke the connection. He clasped their palms together, unable to hide the trembling.

Using his favorite word from earlier, she rasped, "brace," then pulled him into the waterfall.

Unsurprising, the deluge forced her down and did its best to drown her. It tried to rip their hands apart, but his squeeze became painful, keeping them together.

He attempted to pull her backward, but she fought to press forward. Not trusting her, he yanked, agonizing her abused muscles.

She countered, twisting to jerk him with both hands. Precious air disappeared from her lungs, burning for her to surface. With one final heave, she won the battle. The torrent on her head lessened, and she flung her other hand out, stroking it through the water to help her rise.

She shot upward, gagging and coughing.

"Woofwoofwoof." Waffles hacked and sneezed.

Water splashed with Troy's grand entrance. He sucked

in air and swiped at his face, dislodging the material over his nose and mouth. Piercing blue eyes latched onto hers, flaming. "Are you trying to kill me?" he sputtered, coughing. "Is this revenge?"

She raised an eyebrow. Waiting. His concussion made him a little slow to put the pieces together, but she understood. Her brain was in the same boat.

"Ruff. Ruff. Ruff." Waffles stood in a shallow section, wagging his tail.

Troy snapped his attention on the dog, then froze, his mouth dropping open.

Bingo. She couldn't stop the goofy smile from spreading. The bruises on her face protested, but they didn't dampen the moment.

His gaze shifted to his left, and he blinked. A lot.

The inferno's color show still shone on the cave-covering waterfall. The fire's glow penetrated enough to cut into the darkness, but not enough to read a book.

Thundering water reverberated throughout the stone cave, drilling into her ears. Her eyes were still irritated, sore, and itchy, the river unable to heal the damage from the smoke's particles. The rest of her senses worked fine. Sort of. About as fine as a bomb and strangling survivor could expect.

An epiphany smacked the side of her head. She'd come a long way from the terrified woman crawling on the floor from the sound of a gunshot. So much had happened since then, that moment felt like a lifetime ago. She wasn't signing up to become a police detective like Troy, but her tolerance for handling frightening situations had increased tenfold.

"Is this real?" *Plink, plink, plink, plink.* Water rivulets ran to the hem of his shorts, partial T-shirt, and extremities to drop into the stream like discordant instruments.

"Yes." She snatched the face covering down. Dank, earthy, mineral-choked air infiltrated her body. She wanted to hug it.

"My miracle." A slow grin split Troy's cracked lips. The helpless failure and despair dripped away with the water, allowing him to stand taller. "God granted my miracle."

The importance of his declaration seeped in. "You prayed?" She forced her damaged larynx to work. "Asked...miracle?" That was a far cry from the angry man who insisted only dumb luck and not God helped them stay alive.

Red flared on his cheeks as he looked away.

"That's...awesome." She closed the distance and hugged him. He stiffened, then relaxed. "Faith?"

His arms encircled her. "Not restored." He correctly interpreted her one-word question. "But I'm working on it."

A wet furry body pressed against their legs. The tip of Waffles's wagging tail smacked her butt.

Troy crouched and hugged the dog. "I thought I lost you, big guy."

Waffles danced and bobbed his head until he found skin to lick. Troy laughed, roughing the dog's fur. The warm, deep sound hit her in the heart. For too many minutes, she thought she'd never hear it again.

Tears edged her eyes. In the last hour, she'd experienced so many emotions. Too many. From believing she'd die to knowing they escaped, and the terrifying moments between, which sapped her energy. She wanted to sleep for days but knew, even if she had the chance, she wouldn't be able to rest.

Too much had happened too quickly to process it all. And they weren't completely safe yet. The psychopath was still a threat. He was like a cockroach able to survive the apocalypse. She had no doubt he'd strike again. They also had to find a way to alert the firefighters they needed help. And a hospital. And food. And, and, and…

Grasping Troy's shoulder, she got his attention. "Follow." She motioned toward the darkness. "Cavern."

Chapter Thirty-Seven

Troy opened the pack strapped on Waffles's back. It had shifted but still remained secured to the dog. Fishing inside, he grabbed the flashlight. Rubber encased the entire device, and the heft spoke of industrial use. This wasn't something found in a discount store. Psychopath had paid good money for it. And they would reap the benefit.

Clicking it on, Troy admired the strong, bright beam illuminating a large swath. With the extra batteries, they should have no problem navigating.

"Treasure." Nicole stroked her purple-and-black throat, the handprints vivid. "Have...fire department—" Her hoarse voice gave out.

He understood. She wanted to find whatever her uncle hid inside the cavern. They'd already have it when they finally escaped the mountain. No need to come back. He didn't know about her, but he hoped he never set foot on this property again.

Rising, he aimed the beam toward the yawning darkness. The river had constricted on this side of the waterfall, no longer fifteen feet wide. Now it was about eight. More like a deep stream than river. Jagged stone walls rounded at the top. Narrow ledges existed between the water and sides in sections. Sharp points intermittently grew from the low ceiling—nowhere close to the impressive stalactite levels seen in pictures. Hopefully that'd appease Nicole. If the stream remained at this depth, they could walk without hunching, but there was no guarantee.

He did not want to speak ill of God's miracle, but he

prayed they wouldn't have to stay in the water. They had traded mind-melting heat for a cool tunnel that promised to become colder as they progressed deeper into the mountain. They'd already experienced the low-sixties temperature and that was with dry clothes. The three of them were soaking wet and a long way from drying. They'd be lucky if they escaped without pneumonia. He wasn't looking to add more misery to his already long list.

Waffles trotted ahead, balancing on the narrow edge.

"I heard water the last time we entered the cavern." Troy trudged forward. The current wasn't as strong, and now he understood why. The waterfall had added the tremendous force.

Nicole fell in step beside him. The flashlight's beam reflected off the stone, illuminating them in a low light.

The cascading deluge behind them echoed, drowning out almost everything, but he didn't miss the wheeze in her laboring breaths.

"Do you need me to carry you?"

She glared at him, her eyebrows furrowing at severe angles.

He held up his free hand in surrender. "I come in peace."

The scowl deepened.

"You're not weak." He bounced his gaze between the enraged woman and the unknown ahead. "That's not why I'm offering. Okay?"

No response if he didn't count the death stare.

"Stop visualizing throwing rocks at my head." He mock-glowered.

Her lips twitched as she spread her hands apart.

"You're throwing boulders. Got it." He rolled his eyes. "Are you done?"

She shook her head.

He chuckled. This woman amazed him. She kept rolling with the punches, and they had some serious blows, and still found a way to joke.

The river cut a swath to the left. The rounding at the top of the walls steepened, forcing him to walk behind her so he didn't impale his head.

"I don't know how you're still moving." He eased beside her the second the tunnel allowed. "You ate one energy bar too long ago to count. Your body needs sustenance to heal, and with all we've been through, a Thanksgiving feast wouldn't be enough."

Waffles disappeared beyond the light.

"All I'm offering is a time-out from walking. A way to conserve your strength—"

She lightly smacked his biceps, then jabbed a finger at him.

"I won't insult you and say I'm fine." It didn't take a genius to read her sentiments. "I'm just better than—" He chuckled, scratching the corner of his runaway mouth. "Not finishing that sentence. You'll brain me for sure."

She nodded. Emphatically.

"Right." He cleared his throat, then winced at the burning. "Back to what I started to say before. I heard water when we were in the cavern, but we have no clue if this is the same stream."

"Odds…high." Wheeze, wheeze.

"True." He masked his wince for her. She was clinging to pride by her fingernails. "But this could branch—"

Another arm whap.

"Don't borrow trouble." He snorted. "Now you sound like my mother."

She raised an eyebrow.

"For someone not talking, you're saying *a lot*."

One regal nod.

He was so gone on her. No ifs, ands, or buts. She had

wormed her way into his heart. No, his soul. Falling? No, he'd *fallen* in love.

"I like," she croaked, "your mother."

"Oh, she'd love you. Trust me." He pretended a horrified shudder. Okay, so maybe he didn't pretend. The realization he'd fallen for Nicole hit him in the solar plexus. "Chase?" He rocked his hand in an it-could-go-either-way gesture.

"Twin." She mimed eating out of the palm of her hand.

"I bet you dominate on charades night."

She huffed on her broken and dirt-encrusted nails, then buffed them on a tattered sleeve.

"Your humbleness is one of the things I like about you, Witten."

The light banter helped him block the plummeting temperature. His goose bumps had grown cities featuring hotels and high-rises. His teeth tried to chatter, but talking put his mouth to better use. And kept him from freaking out.

He couldn't be in love with Nicole. That was crazy. Impossible. He must still be high on escaping a horrid death. His endorphins made him love everything right now. That was all.

His soul didn't buy a word he tried selling. It offered a visceral memory of his heart shattering when he thought they were about to die.

Yeah, but—

A second, fully immersive replay of his yearning for the storybook future with Nicole blasted in his mind.

But he couldn't love her.

A third offering included this thought: their time left was measured in minutes, not years.

Oh, Lord. He *had* fallen in love with her.

What did he do now?

Nothing, his practical mind answered. *Absolutely nothing.* Escaping the mountain was the first and only priority.

Everything else took a back seat. He had to continue like nothing earth-shattering happened. Once they were safe, maybe he'd tell her.

The stream babbled just like the riddle described, and he hoped for Nicole's sake she discovered whatever her uncle left behind. For his sake, he wanted it to remain a mystery. Until this moment, he hadn't understood the quandary it put him in. The FBI's search warrant covered everything Ross Witten owned. Troy had never gotten the chance to notify them about the retreat center. Had they stumbled onto a connection by now? Maybe. But that didn't absolve him of his duty. As a sworn police officer, he had a responsibility to inform the FBI about the property and anything Ross hid on it, like the "treasure."

Splashes ahead had him focusing the light into as many crevasses as possible.

Waffles trotted forward with his mouth open. The dog's lungs wheezed like his owner's. He had gone too long without a snout covering. Ash, noxious fumes, and other toxic particles rattled in the Swissador's respiratory system. He needed a vet. ASAP. Troy banked on convincing a firefighter to treat the dog as critically as a human. Troy hadn't met a fellow first responder yet who didn't love animals— some preferred them over people.

"Woof. Woof." Waffles splattered cold water up their legs with his rapid stop.

"Thanks, buddy." He didn't lower the flashlight. The darkness stretched for…however long, and the rock tunnel remained a hazard if they didn't watch their step—or heads.

Troy's wish to walk on dry land remained unfulfilled. His prayer for this stream to be linked to the one in the cavern started gnawing at his gut. They had trudged against the current—it may not be as forceful, but it was still present—

far longer than their previous time in the tunnels. Had they passed the moonshine distillery? Not literally. But were the stills on the other side of one of the walls? Shiners needed water to make the hooch, and underground setups were only successful near abundant sources. Like this one. So, how did the stream connect to the cavern? *Did* this stream flow into the cavern?

Nicole's labored breathing pulsed against the stone. She tried to hide it, but it was no use. The stone reverberated everything.

"Take a break?" He held his breath, bracing for a whack on his arm or head.

"No." She motioned to the dog. "Show us…" Coughing bent her over.

He rubbed her back, sending soothing vibes into his palms. *God, please don't let the rattle in her lungs be pneumonia.* The prayer came easier. Especially since it was for Nicole.

"Show," she croaked through an enormous hack. Stuttering an inhale, she straightened. "Waffles."

The dog understood her pantomime. He pivoted, tossing more icy water on them.

"He did that on purpose." Troy didn't feel like joking, but he was helpless to do something as she struggled.

"Told…him…to." She pointed to her mind.

"So." He hovered beside her slow steps. "You have ESPN now?"

"Can't—" inhale "—watch Orioles… Ravens…highlights without."

He loved her quick wit. She didn't miss a beat. "Groaaaannn," he drew out. "We have to convert you to Phillies and Eagles, stat."

Snort. Her hand rubbed her heaving chest. "I'm…good."

"Debatable."

Her elbow found his ribs. His very sore and bruised ribs. Hiding the sharp hiss of pain by snickering, he made a production of spotlighting the dog.

"What do you think he found?" His question was rhetorical.

"That," she answered anyway, pointing.

Waffles stood where the stream split into two.

Chapter Thirty-Eight

Nicole longed for the break Troy suggested. She needed to stop. Her lungs were burning and felt too big for her chest. No matter how hard she regulated her breathing, it rattled and labored.

No doubt Troy heard it. It was probably the reason he offered. As much as she wanted to sit, the moment she did, she was done. Better to keep going and find a way out of this nightmare. After she unearthed whatever her uncle left for her.

She never wanted to see this property again. If they didn't find it today, it would have to wait years before she came back, if ever. As much as she wanted something positive from her uncle, her Survival Bucket List meant more. A beach with no forest nearby was in her future.

Troy shifted the flashlight down the left channel. Nothing new. Water flowed their way within a natural tunnel. The right branch was similar but not as wide.

Whatever had consumed Troy's thoughts still hadn't let go. Fish darted out of the light beam, and he didn't react. For a while, she could almost see the wheels turning, and now it clung to him like an extra burden. She opened her mouth to ask but had the feeling she'd be intruding.

Waffles saved her from deciding whether to press or not. He turned, his tail brushing Troy in the process. Without hesitating, he trotted down the right fork.

Oh, Lord. Was he leading them to more explosives? Then again, his sensitive nose might smell the ethanol in the cavern. The very place she needed to find. Not having a reason to choose the other branch, she followed Troy, who trailed Waffles, the stream not wide enough to walk abreast.

The water babbled, occasionally splashing up the sides of the striated walls. Mineral sparkles twinkled in the flashlight beam, dazzling them like an underground galaxy. Her bruised brain urged her to pause and study the configuration. Were there constellations? That'd be amazing.

"I doubt it."

She startled at Troy's answer. Had she spoken the crazy question out loud? Seemed like her concussion amused itself inwardly and vocally.

"But it'd be fun to make up new ones." Troy raised a wet finger and pressed water against a sparkle, then drew a line to another. By the time he reached the fourth, moisture had dried from his skin. "Oh, well. I tried."

Yes, he had. She snickered—unable to fully laugh—at the wonky shape that resembled nothing.

No two ways about it, he'd burrowed into her soul. She thought for sure she didn't have the capacity to open her heart after her uncle's loss, but Waffles and Detective Troy Hollenbeck proved her wrong. She'd fallen for them both, er, in different capacities.

At any other time, that bombshell would have sent her reeling. Would've had her analyzing every angle, and consulting friends, but she didn't have it in her. She'd fallen in love with Troy. Shocking, terrifying, and so quick. She didn't know basic first-date information like his favorite movie genres, if he read books, or his preferred junk food—and he had to like high-calorie goodies or she'd drive him nuts. And supremely important: Did he hog the remote?

Then again, fighting for survival taught her more than a slew of dates ever could. She trusted him implicitly. He doubted himself, but he had her complete faith. Her uncle made her believe he was a great man, and she wrestled with accepting otherwise, but Troy was honorable down to his bones. She knew it. *Felt* it. He'd never do anything to betray her or be duplicitous.

She should probably mention something to him, but without her larynx, pantomiming this kind of revelation didn't work. It was better to wait.

Waffles halted, one paw lifted. His tail froze as his ears pricked forward. He sniffed. Sniffed again. *"Grooooooow-wwwwwwl."* He took off.

"Waffles," Troy snapped, taking off, too. "Stop."

The dog didn't slow.

Begging her body to run, she pressed a hand against her wheezing chest. She was enrolling that mutt into obedience school for sure.

"Nicole," Troy commanded between heavy breaths, "stay behind me."

She hadn't forgotten his preference. And right now it wasn't a problem. The narrow stream didn't offer her a chance to plow ahead of him.

Waffles disappeared beyond the light.

Troy vanished with the light.

Nicole sloshed through the waist-high water trying not to panic. Where did they go? Throwing a hand out, she scraped along the wall. Her fingers quickly tingled from the rough rock. The bend explained the disappearances.

Farther ahead, Troy chased the dog. If she didn't pick up the pace, she was going to lose all illumination. Chills blasted her veins. Her wicked imagination took root. Fish swimming in the water was one thing, but what about snakes?

Nope. Nope. Nope. Energy poured into her legs. She'd pass out later with Troy and Waffles on guard for the slithering serpents.

As she closed the distance, her eyes played tricks on

her. Her blood must be more oxygen starved than she realized. Faint orange flickered ahead.

No. Flashbacks of the raging inferno grabbed her tight. Fire. Heat. Death. The crackle and snap rang inside her head.

Can't be, a tiny voice attempted to cut through the horror. She clung to that voice. Why couldn't it be? She concentrated on the answer. The roaring fire tempered to the background.

Black dots grew into blobs, obscuring vision. She had to slow her pace. She had to catch Troy and Waffles.

Explosives. The answer popped into mind. If the fire had infiltrated the tunnels and reached the cavern, it would've exploded. She, Troy, and Waffles would be dead. Obviously, they weren't. So…

What was the orange light? The closer she reached, the brighter it grew.

The tunnel plunged into darkness except for the unexplained light.

Nicole instantly stopped. Instinct drove her to tread forward carefully. She didn't understand why at first, but then it hit her. Waffles hadn't made a sound since he first started running, and she didn't hear movement from Troy. In fact, silence prevailed.

Heart slamming against her ribs, she advanced. The desert growing in her mouth couldn't stop the wheeze uttering past her lips. She cut off the noise with a wet hand.

What happened to the flashlight?

Step by slow step she pushed through the water.

Where was Troy? Waffles? Had they found another fork in the stream? Why leave her behind?

Fear slunk up her spine, wrapping around her battered throat and squeezing her swollen lungs. Troy wouldn't abandon her without a good reason. Neither would Waffles. She clung to the surety while at the same time doubting it.

If they didn't ditch her, where did they go? Had they fallen into a trap? No. One of them would alert her. Then what? Questions with no answers dogged her.

Right foot. Left foot. She eased through the water. One hand "saw" with her fingertips, the other was losing the battle to mask her labored breathing.

Tension coiled, curling and twisting until she wanted to scream.

The stream gurgled, flowing past her, unfazed by the building suspense.

Splash behind her. She jumped, yelping into her palm and whirling sideways. Darkness hid the perpetrator. Throwing stealth to the wind, she started running against the water.

The orange light grew brighter as she closed the distance. It wasn't as steady as she first believed. It flickered and shifted…like flames. *No. No. No.* Primal fear seized control.

A shadow separated from the side of the wall, growing larger, blocking the only light.

A scream lodged into her throat. Unmitigated terror threw her body backward. Her feet slipped out from beneath her, and she landed in the stream on her spine.

Vises clamped around her forearms. She fought, jerking this way and that to shake the hold. The vises tightened. No. Escape. Fight. Break free. Her primal brain didn't care who or what it fought as long as she won.

Her eyelids flew open. Cold water and darkness filled her vision. Her cheeks puffed as her lungs screamed for air. *Oh, God, please.* She had to surface. Jamming her feet against the bottom, she pushed.

Her body shot upward. Her muddled brain couldn't keep up with the sudden changes. Seconds behind, she realized the vises no longer gripped her arms. Something bent her forward, then hammered her back.

Hacking, she ejected icy water.

"…breathe. Slow down."

What? Who? Gagging took precedence. Once she finally expelled the last of the stream water and managed a shuttering breath, she tuned in to her senses. They instantly recognized the shadowy figure. Troy. She slumped.

Terror had convinced her to act irrationally. Her hindbrain controlled her actions, reducing her to fight or flight. No mauling animal, venomous snake, or psychotic human attempted to kill her. *Of course* Troy had been the shadow. Who else was in the tunnel?

"Awwwwwwww," a voice she prayed to never hear again mewed. "Isn't this touching?"

Chapter Thirty-Nine

Troy snapped his head around, tightening his hold on Nicole. He couldn't fathom what had terrified her to the point of fighting like a banshee, but now he had a clue.

"Woofwoofwoof. Grrooooooowwwwwwl." Waffles positioned his big body between his humans and the threat. The scruff on the back of his neck rippled.

The orange glow behind obscured the psycho's face. Troy snatched the flashlight sticking out of his side pocket and clicked it on.

"Been helping yourself to my stuff, I see." The psycho stood in the center of the stream. The dirty bandage wrapping on his left arm was prevalent through the tattered remains of the man's sleeve. Waffles left his mark.

"You're helping yourself to mine." Troy motioned to the Beretta clutched in the man's hand.

The madman grinned. "I think I got the better end of the deal."

So did Troy. He had hoped to recover his gun when they found the cavern. An officer who failed to keep track of his weapon didn't deserve to wear the badge. The weapon meant to protect himself and innocents was about to be used against them.

"We have some unfinished business." The psycho focused on Nicole. "Your boyfriend can't save you this time." His aim shifted to her chest. "You're surrounded by fire. You can't run. You can't hide."

"Neither can you." Troy tightened his arm over the back of her shoulders.

The madman scoffed. "We'll see." Using the gun, he gestured toward the cavern. "We're all going to walk inside nice and easy. No tricks. No attacking dogs. Nothing." His fake congenial expression dropped, revealing the lethal predator. "Anyone does *anything* other than what I say, dies."

A shiver stole through Nicole, echoing Troy's. The psychotic man meant every word. Twice the three of them had gone up against this man, and twice the man had lost. His radar would be oversensitive to the point of a hair-trigger. Troy had to bide his time. Play this smart. Lull the criminal into a false sense of security. Whatever it took to separate Nicole and Waffles from danger.

The psycho didn't turn around. He walked backward, keeping the Beretta leveled on Nicole. Waffles's muscles remained stiff, and his focus trained on the threat. The dog might not follow a basic command like "stop," but he had his priorities straight. Protect his human.

The stream continued through a rounded opening similar to the one found behind the waterfall, though the entrance dropped to three feet. Not easy to navigate and keep the gun in sight. Waffles popped through with no issues.

No wonder Troy hadn't seen the stream the first time around. It was tucked on the far side of the cavern, opposite of where they first came in. Three vintage lanterns had been lit and hung on large iron nails at various points in the oversize cavern. The high ceiling was still in shadows, so Troy blasted the darkness with the flashlight. Menacing stalactites grew. Long mineral formations covered most of the apex. Troy guessed the floor probably had stalagmites, but the moonshiners cleared them out to build their enterprise.

"Turn that off and throw it over there." Psycho pointed at an empty section. "Don't want you getting *bright* ideas to use it as a weapon."

It had crossed Troy's mind. He clicked the flashlight off and tossed it into the indicated spot.

"You're going to climb out—" the madman's fingers on the gun's grip adjusted "—one at a time. Cop, hold the dog. He twitches in my direction, I shoot him."

Waffles snarled as if understanding the threat.

Yep. The dog definitely had his priorities straight. Troy hoped Waffles got the chance to scar the madman with another set of bite marks. The guy deserved nothing less after leaving bruises on Nicole's throat.

The criminal stomped on the stones edging the stream's sides, using them like stairs to exit.

"You first." The Beretta motioned to Nicole.

She inhaled, her lungs rattling worse than before. Planting a cross-trainer onto a rock, she threw her arms out to keep her balance, then found the next step.

"Don't move," Psycho snapped, aiming the gun at Troy's forehead.

Troy froze, his hand inches from helping Nicole.

"She climbs out by herself."

"I'm…okay," she rasped, offering Troy a tremulous smile. Turning, she completed the trek and stood where the madman pointed.

"Take the backpack off the dog." The man pointed toward the flashlight. "Throw it there."

Troy did as told just to move this along. He was tired of shivering in cold water.

"I found this—" Psycho held up a bundle of twine "—while I was searching. Tie the dog to the still, then move five feet to the left."

Troy caught the rancid rope and led Waffles to a two-foot-tall-and-wide round tub with an iron strap binding it together. Sludgy water reeking of vinegar kept the basin from moving. He fashioned a knot that looked impressive, but Waffles could easily escape if he tugged hard enough. Troy prayed the dog wouldn't break free too soon. It was a risk, but he needed all the help he could get.

Nicole stood six feet on his right, next to desecrated barrels and crates spilling molded straw and littering broken wood pieces. Grimy glass and pottery jugs cluttered the floor, most toppled over.

"You've been thorough in your search." Troy studied the mess encompassing the entire cavern. The guy hadn't just been searching. He'd ransacked everything.

The criminal shifted to stand equidistant from Troy, Nicole, and Waffles with his back to the oversize still.

"Where is it?" The madman swung the gun toward Nicole's chest.

Her arms instantly crooked at the elbows, raising her hands in surrender. "I—I…don't know."

The psycho racked the Beretta's slide. Since Troy always kept a bullet in the chamber, the madman just ejected the extra shot. But the chilling sound did its job. Nicole jumped, blood draining from her face.

"Don't test me." He raised the weapon, aiming at her forehead.

"I—I'm not." She coughed, her chest heaving up and down.

"Your voice is nasty." Psychopath's gaze traced the bruises on her throat in the shape of his hands. He grinned. "Wonder if it's permanent." Evil widened the dark smile. "I should kill you and call it mercy."

Nicole winced, unable to hide the tremble.

Troy's teeth protested clenching, same as his palms with his fingernails biting into flesh.

"Grroooowwwwlllll." Waffles lowered her head, stretching the twine as far as it would reach.

Troy held his breath, willing the dog to stop. He did.

Psycho glanced at Waffles, then Troy before focusing on Nicole. "We'll discuss mercies later. You said the answer was moonshine."

So, the criminal had been close enough to hear them discuss the riddle. The muscle in Troy's jaw twitched. If only he'd known.

"Yes," she wheezed, nodding.

"What else?" The madman lowered his aim to her heart. "I missed the other two answers."

Ah. That was how the guy beat them here. He'd left before the fire had driven Troy, Nicole, and Waffles into the river. The guy had probably used the tunnel entrance they missed. He'd had the map long enough to know the landmarks to locate.

"Stream," she rasped. "Cave...or...tunnel."

Psycho's brows slammed down. "What's that mean?"

"The treasure's in the moonshine cavern's stream," Troy barked, unable to stay quiet another second. Nicole was a strong woman, but she hadn't been trained to stare down the barrel of a gun held by a madman. Not that Troy had ever dealt with a true psychopath. But he wanted the focus off her as much as possible.

The criminal glanced at the stream peacefully flowing into and out of the cavern. "Find it."

Troy took a step.

"Not you." The Beretta pointed at Troy's heart. "Her."

Nicole flinched. Lowering her hands, she turned toward the water.

"She needs help." It killed Troy to be separated from her. He needed to be closer in case, *when*, this all went south.

"I'm...fine." Nicole wobbled descending into the water. She bit her lip, glancing left, then right at the bottom. "Light."

"I'll hold the flashlight." Troy began moving, not giving the psycho a chance to intervene.

The criminal jogged away from the still, depriving Troy the chance to jump him.

Troy snatched the flashlight and strode to Nicole. Clicking it on, he illuminated the stream.

"Don't enter the water." The criminal's command rankled Troy.

"Fine." He knelt on the side, ignoring the cool rock floor digging into his bruised knees.

In silence, he and Nicole worked together. Troy's smoke-damaged eyes still weren't clear, making it harder to spot details that seemed out of place.

They'd started on the far left, scouring steadily to the right. Troy's shoulders ached, his neck was sore, and his head throbbed. He couldn't imagine how Nicole was faring in the icy water. But it was better than the raging inferno.

"Troy."

He blinked her into focus. Mentally kicking himself for losing concentration, he readjusted the flashlight. "See something?"

She pointed.

Below him, a grouping of stones was cleaner than they should be. Mud and slime coated everything else except for this two-by-one-foot section. The stones weren't pristine. Sediment and silt had had time to begin covering the rocks, but not to the depth of the others.

They found the treasure.

Chapter Forty

Nicole stared at the stones. Her uncle's last treasure hunt had come to an end. Behind those rocks was something precious. She wasn't referring to monetary value. Uncle Ross had taken time to carefully craft the riddle that led her to this place. This moment. She'd never solve his puzzles again.

A tear tracked down her cheek. As she fingered the edge of a stone, her heart broke. No matter what she learned about her uncle, she had this. This cherished connection no one else experienced.

"Stop stalling," the psychopath snapped, intruding on her grief. "Dig it out."

The muscle in Troy's jaw ticked.

In the gap between Troy's arm leaning near the stream's edge and Psychopath's legs, she watched Waffles pulling on the filthy twine.

Lowering her attention to the rocks, she clenched her teeth. That madman didn't deserve whatever her uncle buried. The treasure was special for her. She doubted it contained anything valuable beyond building a loving memory. And this...*man* desecrated that.

"I don't need two of you to recover it."

The menace in the threat chilled her blood. Her eyes snapped up to find him leveling the gun on Troy's back. Coward.

She snatched at the first stone to reach her fingers. It remained in place. Wiggling and prodding finally had it shifting. *Pop.* It broke free along with a plume of silt mucking the water. The rest of the rocks were easy to clear.

Dropping the last onto the pile in the center of the stream, she crouched to see what waited inside the hole. At first, she didn't see anything. Of course, her vision hadn't been clear since the smoke.

Her hand trembled as she reached inside. Trying not to imagine snakes or other creepies attacking her, she curled her fingers around something thin and solid. Tugging, she pulled the object out. And almost dropped it. It was *heavy*.

Smarting at the pulled shoulder muscle, she lifted. A black handle was attached to… "What…is it?"

The item was fifteen inches high, sixteen inches wide, and seven inches deep. It also had a lock requiring a key near the handle.

Troy's brows furrowed. "There's writing…" He leaned closer. "I think it's a safe." His thumb scraped across a label, clearing the muck. "Yeah. Fireproof and waterproof."

"Hand it over." Psycho shifted his aim to her. "Now."

Nicole's world narrowed onto the ominous round hole at the end of the barrel.

"Your uncle stole from my father." The madman's dark eyes spewed hatred. "*You* handed over what should have been *mine*. Now I'm stealing what's yours. Your uncle owes me a treasure. That—" he pointed at the safe dangling from her fatigued arm "—will have to do."

Troy clutched both sides of the "treasure," relieving her trembling muscles.

"Don't play the hero, Cop." The madman glanced at Troy. "It won't work this time. Set that on the ground and back away."

"After I help Nicole—"

"Not what I said." The weapon swung twenty degrees to target Troy's chest not covered by the safe. "Put it down. Walk away."

The skin on Troy's fingers whitened from his tightening hold. He set the safe on the floor beside the stream, then stood.

So many things happened at once: the knot holding Waffles snapped free, the dog snarled, charging Psychopath, the madman started to twist, Troy grabbed her wrists, and Waffles lunged. Straight at Psycho.

The madman threw his left arm up in defense.

Troy yanked upward, almost dislodging both her shoulders.

Waffles slammed into the man, his sharp canines sinking into the bandaging.

Psychopath stumbled backward, screaming and jerking his arm.

Troy ripped her from the stream, her shins scraping the stones as he pulled her out.

Waffles hung on, snarling and thrashing. His back paws took advantage of the uneven rock flooring. He found leverage and tackled the madman.

Nicole managed to plant her feet on the floor and save her shoulder sockets.

Psycho screamed, keeping Waffles's teeth from transferring to his throat. He swung the gun up.

"Don't!" Nicole freed her tangled arms to save her dog.

"Nicole," Troy shouted.

The weapon's true aim registered.

Throwing herself sideways, she smacked into Troy.

Crack. Gunfire echoed.

"No!" Troy howled. "Please, God, *no.*"

Troy toppled to the floor, Nicole's deadweight driving him to land hard. His head smacked into the safe, hitting the concussion lump. Stars floated through his dazed mind as blackness took hold.

Menacing growls and yelps trickled in from far away.

Get up, his adrenaline demanded. The fuzz in his brain had trouble processing the order.

Get. Up. Now.

Troy rolled to his hands and knees.

Nicole flopped to the rock floor. Her eyes remained closed.

"Nicole," he cried hoarsely.

A loud yip of pain broke through the haze.

Waffles. Psychopath. Gun. Troy's jaw clenched. The man still had Troy's Beretta. Forcing his gaze to sharpen, he found Waffles struggling to subdue the criminal.

The madman raised the weapon.

With a battle cry that barely verbalized, Troy leaped. Ignoring every wound and injury, he charged forward and kicked the man's hand. The Beretta hit the rock floor, skittering away. Dropping to his knees, he punched the madman in the temple. The guy's head snapped to the side, and he stopped moving.

"Waffles, release," Troy commanded, fighting the rising nausea. Double vision plagued his sight as the pounding headache exploded.

Psycho's arm flopped onto his stomach, dropping from Waffles's open mouth. The steady rise and fall of the chest assured Troy the man wasn't going to die soon.

Waffles keened, darting for Nicole.

Troy forced his vision to clear enough to make it to her side.

Her eyes remained closed.

"Nicole." He plopped a foot into the stream, maneuvering to cradle her head into his lap. "Wake up."

Blood flowed from her left side. Too much blood pooled onto the ground. Lifting his face, he howled. "You should've taken *me*." Fury burned inside every cell. "She's innocent. She doesn't deserve this—"

"Troy…"

The soft word refocused his attention. Gray eyes peered up at him with so much agony in their depths.

"Hey." He gently smoothed hair off her face. "Stay with me, okay?" His tears hit her nose and cheeks.

Waffles whined, lying beside his human.

"I'm...sorry."

Her apology slayed him. "I'm the one who's sorry. I—"

"No." She coughed, and her abdomen rippled, agitating the open wound. "You matter." Her breathing shallowed, and she winced. "You're...important."

"Don't talk." She needed to use her energy for healing instead of on empty platitudes.

Her brows furrowed. "Heroes." A finger lifted an inch to point at him, then the dog. "God's...blessings."

From his point of view, he was anything but.

"My miracles." Her eyes closed.

"Hey. Stay with me, and I'll give you a reward."

Her eyelids fluttered.

"I really like you." He attempted to grin. "I mean, I showed up with a humongous bag of dog food." He rubbed his chin. "I pretty much used Waffles as an excuse for a date."

Waffles lifted his head. It cocked left, then right.

"We...accept." Her face lost animation. "I'm cold."

Terror seized his heart.

Waffles jumped to his paws. He sniffed Nicole, then took off. His tail disappeared on the other side of the still, aiming for the tunnel they originally traversed.

Gazing back at Nicole, he found her eyes closed. "No. Hey." His heart slammed into his chest. "Wake up."

Her eyelids fluttered again. "Promise me." The words were so weak. "You keep...that...safe." She pointed at the "treasure." A large shiver wracked her.

He held her chilled hand. "I promise."

Her head drooped to the side as she passed out.

Chapter Forty-One

Troy bent over from the sob wrenching his body. He tried to scream. Tried to yell. Nothing came out.

Don't leave me. The words howled in his head.

Nicole's chest rose and fell, but it was not strong. Her damaged lungs weren't processing enough air. Blood still seeped from the wound.

Cover it. His training offered the advice, and he wanted to beat himself for not binding her earlier. Stupid concussion.

Tearing off his T-shirt, he plunked it in the water. He wasn't sure if he was about to hurt her more by using it as a bandage—

The backpack had a first-aid kit.

Gently setting her head on the floor, he raced for the item. Snatching up the pack, he also gathered his Beretta and the rancid rope.

"Woof. Woof. Woof." Waffles's continuous barks echoed into the cavern.

He snapped his gaze that way. What had the dog found?

Plopping onto the ground, he dumped the bag's contents. He ripped the plastic first-aid box open and plucked out a sterile white wrapping. Wiping his hands on his shirt, he then cleaned the blood from around the wound.

"Ruff. Ruff. Ruff. Woofwoofwoofwoof." Waffles frantically barked.

Hope seared through the grief. *Please, God, send help.*

Wrapping the bandage around her was not easy. He used all three packages. Blood from the floor had transferred onto the bindings from his hands. No matter how hard he tried, he couldn't keep the white pristine. As long as it slowed the bleeding and stopped an infection, it shouldn't matter. *Please, don't let it matter.*

"Wake up," he whispered next to Nicole's ear. "Please, don't leave me."

She didn't react.

"I have so much I need to tell you. So much I want to learn about you."

"Ruffruffruff. Woof. Woof. Woof. Woof."

Troy jammed his Beretta into his holster and quickly tied the psychopath's hands. He did not want to leave Nicole, but he had to investigate Waffles's barking. If a new threat presented itself, he had to know.

Swiping the flashlight off the floor, Troy ran. Well, jogged. Sloppily. The jostling killed his head and ruined his vision. He'd finally stopped seeing double. Though blurriness wasn't a huge improvement.

"Woof. Woof. Woof."

The barks were getting closer.

Having the flashlight made trekking the tunnel easier this second time. It also felt a lot shorter than before. Or maybe he just couldn't stay focused enough to accurately account for time.

The reflectors in Waffles's eyes beamed in the light. He paused barking, studied Troy, then resumed the racket.

"What is it?" Troy realized the dog stood beneath the hole they'd originally fallen through. Detritus still littered the area.

A thump echoed above.

Troy snapped the light upward.

Nothing.

Waffles lifted his two paws as if to stand. His barking became frantic.

It dawned on Troy. Firefighters might be in the cabin.

He picked up an empty multi-gallon bucket and rapped the flashlight end on it. The cacophony echoed and deafened.

Dirt and bits of plywood rained down from the hole. *Yes.* Someone was definitely above.

Come on, he begged. Nicole's life hung in the balance.

Ugly groaning and screeching shot through the tunnel. Troy tossed his bucket and grabbed Waffles's harness.

"Move, big guy." He pulled the dog away from the hole.

Heavy scrape. *Scrape. Scrape.* An inch of light pierced through the ceiling.

Scrape. Scrape. Scrape. More light shone in.

A motor, something like a winch, revved, hefting the dense granite countertops.

In all his years of service, he'd never been so glad to hear that sound.

"Woof. Woof." Waffles remained by Troy's side, staring upward.

"Hello?" a deep male voice yelled. "Someone down there?"

"Yes." Troy's throat burned at the shout, but he didn't care. "Send a medic ASAP. I've got a woman dying of a gunshot wound."

The next couple of minutes stretched his patience. The firefighters had to send someone to get the right gear and EMTs. They also had to outfit an FBI agent in extra turnout pants and jackets to repel the heat as he joined the rescue effort. The man insisted on accompanying the small unit descending into the hole on a portable ladder.

Troy let go of Waffles. The dog sniffed every person, sneezing occasionally. When the dog didn't growl or attack anyone, Troy relaxed for two reasons. One, everyone met the dog's standards—not psychopaths—and two, Troy didn't have to worry about a lawsuit from a bite victim.

Emergency equipment spread among everyone, Troy

and Waffles led the way through the tunnel. Energized now that he had help for Nicole, the trip wasn't as long.

Bursting into the cavern, Troy stepped to the side for the medics to begin working on Nicole. Waffles supervised from feet away.

Nicole jolted awake. Four men and women, two on each side, crowded around her. A hard backboard had been shoved beneath her, killing her spine.

"Lift," a man with a ruddy complexion instructed.

Strain filled the firefighters' faces. Their hats and heavy jackets made it difficult to identify many features. She rose, the world twirling and swaying.

She groaned, nausea making an appearance.

Troy and some man in a suit showing beneath a firefighter jacket hovered next to the psychopath.

"I don't know who he is." Troy's words reached through her team of saviors.

"Julien Renaud," suit man answered. "The appraiser, Richard, woke up in the hospital. Filled us in."

Her team carried her by the backboard.

The psychopath's eyes flew open.

Nicole opened her mouth to shout but was too late.

The madman swept his leg, taking Troy's out from beneath him. Troy slammed onto his back, and the psycho rolled, stopping when he hit Troy. Troy started to get up, but the madman was quicker. He slipped his legs around Troy's neck.

"No." Nicole fought the straps holding her in place.

Gunfire cracked.

The psycho jolted, his legs slackening.

Suit man lowered his handgun. "You okay?"

Troy scrambled out of the hold, falling onto his side. "Yeah."

"Concussion," she mumbled, praying someone in her team heard. Troy was anything but okay.

Her saviors hustled her out of the cavern. At some point, she passed out. She awakened with a stretcher jolting into the back of an ambulance.

"Troy?" She searched, locking onto him inside a second ambulance, its open back facing her.

Blackened tree nubs and smoldering lumps covered the once-thriving forest. Charred stones and a cement foundation remained of the retreat center's main building.

Fire equipment bearing names of many townships were parked throughout. And she overheard more were fighting the fire at different directional points to keep it from spreading any more.

Suit man climbed inside Troy's ambulance—minus firefighter gear—and said something to the detective.

Troy picked up a large black object off the floor.

Her stomach knotted. Troy promised to keep the safe protected. Why did he offer it to suit man?

Suit man pulled a large plastic evidence bag—she'd seen a lot on TV and in movies—from his pocket and snapped it open. Troy fed it inside and suit man sealed it.

Troy must have felt her gaze because his eyes instantly snapped to her. His expression reeked of guilt.

Nicole's heart shattered. Why didn't he wait for her to open the safe? Why didn't he trust her enough to do the right thing if something incriminating was inside? Did he think she'd hide evidence? After everything they'd been through, he should've learned she was an honest person.

Resting against the thin pillow, she stared at the ceiling.

"Your dog's on the way to the vet hospital." An EMT rushed inside as the second uniformed woman slammed both doors shut. Sirens flared to life, and the vehicle began to bump and rock as it hustled from the scene.

Troy Hollenbeck wasn't a criminal hiding in lawful clothing like her uncle, but he'd revealed the duplicity behind the handsome mask.

It just proved she couldn't trust her judgment. She once thought her uncle could never do anything wrong, and look where that got her. A house full of FBI agents telling her about her uncle's illegal history.

She stupidly believed her instincts again when they said she could trust Troy implicitly. That he'd never betray her.

It was time to put this town behind her. She and Waffles would find a home on the beach. The dog was the only companion she needed.

Chapter Forty-Two

Nicole fumbled for the remote tied to the railing on the hospital bed. Unmuting the TV mounted near the ceiling, she forced her painkiller-induced brain to focus.

"...just happening in Chicago," the serious anchor stated as the small video graphic grew to overtake the screen. A live shot of men and women in bulletproof vests with FBI stamped in bold letters hustled two men in handcuffs toward an awaiting SUV. The video changed to another similar tableau with different arrests. Then changed again. And again.

"The FBI swept through Chicago arresting more than fifty people linked to The Syndicate," the anchor informed viewers as the video graphic shrank to show her at a studio desk. "Sources close to the FBI state that indictments such as money laundering, theft, drug trafficking, and illegal weapons dealing have been levied against the head of the crime organization and other members. We'll keep you updated as new information comes in."

The screen cut to the next story. "Bell Edge Police Department Detective Troy Hollenbeck—" a photo of the handsome man in a suit shaking hands with a smiling man filled the top right corner "—was given The Attorney General's Award for Distinguished Service in Community Policing this morning in a ceremony held in the mayor's office—"

Nicole shut the TV off. The vitals monitor spiked, blabbing her broken heart to anyone paying attention. Closing her eyes made everything worse. She couldn't stop seeing his face. Remembering his laugh. Feeling his hand linked with hers.

A lump formed at the base of her throat, pressing on the damaged laryngeal nerve. A surgeon had operated on her voice box, shifting it to improve her chances of talking again. Another surgeon worked on removing the bullet from her side and repairing the damage. She'd been so close to dying from multiple injuries it was a wonder she survived at all. That was a quote the doctors kept repeating as they visited her each day.

Black lungs, swollen throat, bullet wound, infection, and more almost robbed her of life. She was a walking miracle. At least two specialists mentioned publishing a case study about her. Lying alone in a hospital bed, she didn't feel very miraculous. Her mother had camped out for days, but Nicole talked her into going home. Nicole couldn't take another lecture about her scoundrel uncle—though the woman didn't feel that way when she gleefully dropped Nicole off for the summer all growing up.

Tears tracked to the stiff pillowcase. She snatched a tissue from the handy box on the moveable tray table hovering beside her. She'd already gone through two boxes. The nurses had taken pity and supplied her with a name brand that had aloe to save her agitated skin.

She needed Waffles. Her dog would help relieve the crushing heartbreak. More tears coated her cheeks. She thought she'd found "the one." Thought her future included Troy and Waffles—

"Let us pass."

The determined male voice outside the closed door grabbed her attention.

A commotion ensued.

"Woof. Woof."

Her heart leaped. Waffles. She knew that bark.

The door to her private room flew open, banging against the stopper. Waffles darted in. The Swissador raced to her bed, his nails clicking on the tile floor. He went to put the brakes on but slid. His big body shook her bed when he skidded his butt sideways.

Two massive paws plopped onto the edge of her uncomfortable mattress. His big head cocked sideways. *"Woof."*

Tears of a different kind flowed freely. She hadn't seen the dog since they were separated in the rescue. The vet had kept Nicole posted, but it wasn't the same.

Waffles, she mouthed, unable to speak yet. Her left hand buried into his fur, encountering a harness. She wanted to laugh at the formal stitching announcing Waffles was a "Therapy Dog."

Clever. Whoever snuck the dog in knew how to do it right.

No bandages covered fur, and he seemed to be breathing okay. The veterinarian had done an amazing job. Nicole owed that woman a debt of gratitude.

"What's the meaning of this?" a female demanded. Nicole's throat specialist had joined the party just out of sight of her opened door. Nicole saw part of the woman's white coat, scrub pants, and athletic shoes. "Who let that dog into my patient's room?"

Waffles twisted his big head to peer at the tiny woman. He turned back to Nicole. His pink tongue licked Nicole's left forearm.

"I did."

Nicole froze. No. He couldn't be here. Her gaze snapped to the doorway. She had specifically banned Troy from visiting. Her mental health was already a mess. She woke half the floor with her nightmares every time she fell asleep.

"I'm sorry, sir," the man the FBI posted outside her door stated. "I can't let you inside."

The doctor hustled out of the way as the two men in suits jockeyed for position. One blocked, and the other tried to pass.

Troy Hollenbeck. Gorgeous blue eyes lasered onto Nicole, holding her prisoner. Relief, then determination, filled his expression.

"I'm calling security," the doctor announced, motioning toward the nurses' station.

"No one is stopping me from talking to Nicole."

"You're not on the authorized list." Her FBI guard zigged and zagged, countering Troy.

"Nicole." Troy paused, peering over the FBI guy's shoulder. "I'll make a spectacle out here if you don't let me in." He shoved a hand through his hair. "I brought you Waffles. Doesn't that earn me five minutes?"

Waffles whined, his head cocking the other direction. His paw scrapped her thigh as if to say, *Mommy, let Daddy in*.

The FBI man craned his neck. She motioned for the guy to let Troy through.

"Thank you." Troy's shoulders slumped as he visibly exhaled.

"You have *five* minutes." The small doctor pointed a finger up at Troy. "My day's too busy, and I haven't examined her yet." She made a production of looking at her watch.

Troy nodded and strode into the room, slamming the door behind him.

He looked amazing. Clean and official in a charcoal suit with a silk tie that matched his irises, and his detective shield clipped to his belt. The same suit the news just showed. He must've left the ceremony and driven straight here. The bruises on his face and visible sections of his skin were in the end stages of healing. The ugly colors did nothing to detract from his good looks.

Her body itched to jump out of bed and wrap around him like a barnacle. The pieces of her shattered heart bleated.

"I tried calling." He marched around the bed to take a position opposite Waffles. "I've left messages." His hand drove through his hair again. "I had to resort to this." He motioned to Waffles. "But I'm not sorry. I *had* to see you."

She swallowed a large lump of saliva, the surgical swelling preventing her from completing the action. She gagged. Pain blazed through her throat.

The doctor burst through the door. "Out."

"No." Troy moved away from the bed. He leaned against the wall, crossing his arms.

Waffles growled.

"Waffles, come." Troy pointed to the spot beside him.

The dog's front paws hit the tiles, then he trotted to Troy's side.

The doctor blocked Nicole's view as she did her examination. It took more than five minutes for the two of them to settle her throat and the doctor to leave.

Troy hadn't moved an inch.

Fear, guilt, and grief warred for dominance of his expression.

"Are you going to be okay?"

The soft question full of concern paused her wiping her eyes. She rocked her left hand. Maybe. The jury was still out on if she could speak normally again. She'd have to go through physical therapy, and the list of woes continued.

Large hands scrubbed his face. "I'm sorry."

She raised her eyebrows. That apology didn't really say anything.

"Right." He resettled in his previous spot beside the bed. Waffles did the same on the other side.

They both filled the room with their presence. It was too much. It was not enough.

Troy eyed the partially closed door. "I've been told the FBI is turning you over to the US Marshals."

Her eyebrows climbed into her shorn hair. She had been right. The debris and tangled knots were too much to tame. The stylist who graciously offered her services in the hospital room had to cut it short. *Really* short.

"Did you know?"

She nodded. Two men in suits visited this morning, announcing their plan to have the Marshals set her up somewhere safe. Not exactly witness protection, but not left helpless on her own. With the FBI taking down The Syndicate in a coordinated sweep, they feared she'd become a target from those looking for payback. And they wanted her available for future court appearances as needed.

She had a lot of anger and hurt when it came to her uncle, but she also had love. He had collected enough evidence in the form of USBs and documentation to allow the FBI to dismantle or at least cripple the dangerous organization. Their search warrants had yielded nothing. Not a speck of evidence against Ross Witten for any crime. They couldn't prove he buried the sword or had the other stolen museum pieces on the property even though the freshly dug places matched the number of missing items.

But the FBI didn't walk away empty-handed. The treasure she'd found had the evidence—the USBs and documentation—inside.

But how did Troy find out the plan? Only a few people were in the know, or so she thought.

"I'm a detective." His hands curled around the metal side railing, answering her unspoken question. "I made it my business to know. *Especially* something like this."

If he could find out, then what stopped the criminals from locating her?

"Give me some credit." Once again he correctly read her expression. "I'd never do *anything* to put you in danger." His hands strangled the metal. "You can't leave without me."

She blinked at the bold statement.

"I mean it." His piercing blue eyes sharpened. "These last nine days have been torture. You shutting me out has shredded my heart."

Hers, too. Not that she'd tell him that. Plucking the dry-erase board off the mobile table, she uncapped the blue marker. Forced to use her left hand thanks to the cast on her right—she'd broken a bone in the punch—her penmanship left a lot to be desired.

We can't live together. The words were barely legible and not what she wanted to write, but her heart took control.

Troy straightened. "I'll marry you right now if that's the only thing holding you back. I'll have a judge or clergy in ASAP."

Real romantic, she scribbled, scowling.

Troy bent forward, leaving a foot between their faces. "Nicole, I'm telling you I love you."

She blinked, shocked.

"I'm *in* love with you."

The dry-erase board flopped onto her stomach.

"I will marry you this minute."

Her mind scrambled to keep up with the heart pounding against her chest.

"You want me on my knee?" He dropped down.

Waffles did the same, then walked around the bed to stand next to Troy as if supporting.

"Will you marry me?"

Almost everything in her cried yes. It was her dream. What she longed for since falling for this man.

It was wrong.

She snatched the dry-erase board and wrote, *This is not something to joke about.*

His jaw hardened. "I'm not joking."

You lied to me. You betrayed me. You could be doing it again. The slant of the words was in deference to the rising anger. How dare he use her heart against her.

"I'm not lying." He rose. "Just let me explain."

What's there to explain? She flashed the board, then erased. *You promised to keep the safe safe.* Flash. Erase. *Instead—* The word was too big to continue the sentence. She erased. *You gave it to the FBI. You didn't trust me to hand it over myself.* Her underlines smashed the marker against the surface.

His eyes flashed, determination showed bright.

Congratulations on your award. Erase. Her sharp movements shook the bed. *Guess it didn't matter who you stepped on to become the media hero.*

"I. Don't. Care. About. An. Award." His jaw ticked. "I care about *you*." He jabbed a finger at her. "I *love* you."

But not trust. Her hand trembled.

"I do trust you." Troy gripped the rail again. "You're missing a few facts."

She jutted her chin.

"The FBI found the connection between your uncle and that retreat center." His hand thrust through his hair. "They were already obtaining a search warrant when they heard about the fire."

She hadn't known they'd gotten a warrant. Did it change anything? No.

"Your uncle sold multiple properties in Chicago to raise the money to buy the land and develop it."

She had learned that days after her surgery. The lawyer who handled her uncle's affairs called to tell her about the missing paperwork at the time of the will. He'd also mentioned the state of Pennsylvania wanted to buy the land. They planned to restore the forest and turn the bootleggers' tunnels and moonshine cavern into a tourist attraction. She had no problem authorizing the lawyer to begin negotiations on that as well as selling the house and land. As much as it soothed the heartache to learn her uncle bought everything with legitimate money, she wanted nothing to do with any of it. Too many horrible memories were attached to it all now.

Your point?

"The FBI was already on-site. You saw one of their agents save me from Julien Renaud."

The FBI filled her in about Julien and his father, the man who killed the security guards during the museum heist. The senior Renaud was also the inside man for the museum when the robbery happened.

Troy leaned closer. "The FBI agent saw the safe. He demanded it be turned over." His eyes implored her to understand. To believe him. "I tried to hide it, but he caught up to me in the ambulance." Fingers through the hair. "I'm a sworn police officer. I couldn't obstruct justice. I *had* to give it to him even though I knew it would hurt you. I'm sorry."

She bit her lip, tasting salt. She hadn't realized she was crying.

That was my last link to my uncle. Tears hit the board. Erase. *He spent time creating that riddle and hunt.* She wiped the words. *I never got to see inside my final treasure.*

"I'm sorry."

The soft apology felt ripped from his heart. He truly meant it.

"I *do* trust you." Warm hands cupped her cheeks, angling her head to peer at his face. "I *know* you would've turned in the evidence. That's what's hurting most, right? You think I believe you would've covered for your uncle."

She nodded.

"I don't think that. It *never* crossed my mind." He searched her face. "I love you, Nicole. Please, marry me. I can't stand the thought of a future without you. I go where you go."

Her stomach flip-flopped. Her heart burst into song. Her tears and nose leaked.

Grappling for the board and marker without looking, she scribbled, *I love you too*.

Troy pulled back enough to read it.

"Yes," Troy cried, breaking into the happiest, goofiest grin possible. It matched the one on her face.

"Woof." Waffles sat from lying on the floor.

"So, very-soon-to-be Mrs. Hollenbeck. Where are the three of us moving?"

The beach. She underlined until he stole the pen and a long kiss.

* * * * *

Get 4 FREE REWARDS!

We'll send you 2 FREE Books plus 2 FREE Mystery Gifts.

FREE
Value Over
$20

Both the **Love Inspired®** and **Love Inspired®** Suspense series feature compelling novels filled with inspirational romance, faith, forgiveness and hope.